CHANGELINGS

Borgo Press Books by BRIAN STABLEFORD

CHANGELINGS

AND OTHER METAMORPHIC TALES

by

Brian Stableford

THE BORGO PRESS

An Imprint of Wildside Press LLC

MMIX

CONTENTS

CHANGELINGS

INTRODUCTION

There is a school of thought which holds that the aesthetic essence of a story is the change that takes place in the heart and mind of its protagonist. The thesis is not incompatible with the grittier school of thought which holds that the aesthetic essence of fiction is challenge, because it is usually the challenges faced by literary characters that provoke or compel them to change. It must be admitted, however, that there is a very large fraction of popular fiction—just as there is a very large fraction of vulgar real life—that consists of accounts of characters responding to challenges with desperate attempts to patch up a pre-existing reality and protect it, so far as they may, from horrid change. That fraction, of course, reflects the enduring preference of the majority of human beings for the devil they know—the *status quo*—when confronted with any kind of hopeful ambition.

Oddly enough, popular non-fiction contrasts strongly with popular fiction in this respect, largely consisting of various kinds of self-help manuals (including such exhortatory subgenres as gardening books, cookery books and celebrity autobiographies) whose key element is the steadfast assertion of the conviction that every day, in every way, people can get better and better by mobilizing the miraculous power of positive thinking. This discrepancy is probably the best evidence we have of the deadly accuracy of the old adage that although truth is stranger than fiction, fiction is truer—or, to put it another way, the sad truth that while fiction is occasionally hospitable to honest lies, non-fiction consists entirely of dishonest ones.

The principal problem that arises in writing stories in which protagonists do change is figuring out appropriate modes of metamorphosis. Convention offers a series of off-the-peg answers, which are widely reflected in both literature and life, by far and away the most popular being the achievement of exceptional success in matters of love and money. There was a time when every respectable novel ended with a marriage and an inheritance, and every semi-respectable life was expected to feature at least one of each. We live in a different era now, but many people—including writers, who are people of a sort—still feel nostalgic about the old one, even though we all know perfectly well that marriage is a beginning, not an end, and that the only inheritance are currently leaving to our children and grandchildren is a planet so comprehensively fucked-up that it will soon be uninhabitable even by the rich.

In recognition of these embarrassing facts, most of the tales of metamorphosis included herein are ironic black comedies. Some of them feature protagonists who are heroically resistant to change because they are mad, perverse or apathetic; those which feature protagonists avid for change tend to portray such avidity as mad, perverse or artistic. All of the stories are pure fiction, and all of them aspire to be seriously weird, there being no other plausible route to a true aesthetic appreciation of real life. There are fugitive echoes of positive thinking within a few of them, but the collection as a whole is designed to preserve a careful balance between such febrile fanciful follies and the honest virtues of nihilism.

Three of the stories first appeared in *Interzone*, "Changelings" in issue number 85 (July 1994), "The Serpent" in number 99 (September 1995) and "Tread Softly" in number 177 (April 2000). Two first appeared in *Asimov's Science Fiction*, "Inside Out" in the March 1997 issue and "The Oracle" in the May 1999 issue, and two in *Science Fiction Age*, "The Tour" in the January 1998 issue and "Victims" in the January 2000 issue. "Coming to Terms with the Great Plague was first published on the internet at Omni On-Line on December 31, 1997. "After the Stone Age" was first published on the internet at the BBC's Cult TV website on 18 March 2004. "Degrees of Separation" was first published in *The Evil Entwines* by John B. Ford and Friends, Hardcastle (2002).

CHANGELINGS

FRANKIE SAT DOWN at the dressing-table. She placed the open bottle of Armagnac to her right, and the cereal-bowl containing the pills to her left. Between them, mocking and accusatory, sat a blank sheet of paper.

It's not everybody who has a chance to plan their last words, she thought. *This is a privilege. It's an opportunity to be witty and wise, or at least honest. Why don't I have any idea what to write? Am I supposed to be compiling an explanation, an excuse, or a set of insults?*

She picked up the felt-tipped pen that lay beside the empty sheet, and tested the end with her left forefinger, leaving a black smudge. Now she couldn't even die clean.

"Oh, what the hell," she said, speaking aloud although she was well aware of the awful incongruity of taking to an empty room, "it's not as if anyone I love or hate is going to find the bloody thing. It'll only be some fireman or policeman, summoned by a not-very-concerned neighbor when I'm finally missed. That could be weeks away. I'll probably stink so badly that mere words would be utterly superfluous."

She threw the pen over her shoulder without looking to see if it would land on the unmade bed or the ragged rug, and reached out to take a handful of pills. The cocktail included two kinds of barbiturate sleeping pills, two kinds of tranquillizers, two kinds of anti-depressants and some anti-histamines, the last being included as anti-emetics rather than poisons. They were the detritus of thirty-odd prescriptions issued over the last five years. She'd thought about throwing in her paracetamols for good measure but felt, on due consideration, that would have made the medical molehill unreasonably mountainous. She took the first swig of brandy before lifting the pills to her mouth, just to smooth the way, and was still savoring its bite when the doorbell rang.

If that's Jehovah's Witnesses, she thought, *I'll bloody swing for them.*

She sat stock still, waiting to see whether the caller would ring a second time. She didn't make any explicit bargain with herself about what she'd do if there was a second ring, but she understood that some such deal with the treacherous hand of fate was implicit in her hesitation.

At the second ring she let the pills trickle back through her list-less fingers into the bowl. At the third she put the bottle down, and went to answer the door. She flatly and absolutely refused to think anything as stupid as *saved by the bell!* but she was uncomfortably aware of her refusal and all that it signified.

She didn't recognize the man who stood on the balcony; so far as she knew she'd never set eyes on him before. He was far too well-dressed to be a Jehovah's Witness, and she knew he couldn't be a Mormon because Mormons always traveled in pairs. In fact, he was far too well-dressed to be calling on a thirteenth-floor flat in this kind of block, or to be going unaccompanied in this kind of neighborhood. His figure was nondescriptly average and his benign features were soft and pale, but she knew he must be pretty fit be-cause the lifts weren't working and he didn't seem in the least out of breath.

"Excuse me," he said, politely, "but I'm looking for Frances Harrap."

"That's a coincidence," Frankie said, bitterly. "That's who I used to be."

The man looked faintly puzzled, as well he might, but seemed undisturbed by the sharpness of her tone. He simply didn't under-stand what she'd said or the way she'd said it. Frankie was sure that nobody could, even if she tried to explain.

"I'm sorry...," he began.

"That's okay," she said, cutting him off. "What do you want?"

"I'm afraid it will take a little time," he said. "Might I come in, do you think?" He didn't offer his name, let alone any identification, but if he was a con man or a rapist he had the right kind of disguise. Frankie had worked in Debenham's for a while; she knew a three hundred pound suit when she saw it, and she knew the rarity-value of detergent-commercial shirts and neatly-knotted silk ties. In any case, she had nothing to lose, money wise or any other way.

"Sure," she said, opening the door wide and standing back. "I've got all the time in the world. Do you want a cup of tea?"

He blinked. In all probability, she figured, he'd never been of-fered a cup of tea in that tone of voice before. But he wasn't intimidated. In fact, for all his softness and neatness, he somehow didn't look as if he were capable of timidity.

"You're a lucky man," she said, as she pointed him in the direction of the stained MFI sofa. "The staircases are usually full of kids who'd mug you for those shoes, let alone the rest of the gear."

"They probably didn't even notice me," he said, equably. "People usually don't."

"Story of my life," she muttered, as she went into the kitchenette to plug the kettle in. "Sainsbury's Brown Label bags all right?" she called out, half a minute later. "I'm fresh out of Earl Grey."

"Whatever you have," he said, raising his voice no more than was strictly necessary.

"Milk and sugar?"

"Just milk, thank you."

"Perhaps as well—I'm fresh out of sugar too. I spent all this week's housekeeping on posh brandy."

The milk hadn't quite gone off, but she couldn't find it in herself to feel much relief. She splashed it straight on to the tea-bags, because she had recently seen a daytime TV program which assured her that people who cared about appearances never put the milk in first.

She waited in the kitchen for the kettle to boil, then poured the boiling water on. She gave both mugs a quick stir, then squashed the tea-bags against the sides for a few seconds before flipping them into the pedal-bin with practiced ease.

He was waiting patiently. If he'd taken the opportunity to study the living-room closely the experience had not filled him with horror, even though the wallpaper must have been on a par with the stuff that Oscar Wilde had died to avoid. She gave him a point, though, for not nodding in the direction of the paperback-stuffed bookshelves and saying: "Have you read them all?" Previous visitors had assured her that her flat probably had more books in it than all the other flats in the block put together. She always replied—with devastating truthfulness—that they were the horrible proof of the emptiness of her existence.

The anonymous caller sipped tea from his mug without any evident distaste. "I'm afraid," he said, "that what I have to tell you is rather incredible."

"Oh good," she said. "I was afraid you were going to be a bore."

"This may seem to be a peculiar question," he went on, slightly overdoing the apologetic manner, "but do you often feel that you're not like other people—that you're completely out of place in this environment?"

"Oh shit," said Frankie, disgustedly, "you're a fucking Scientologist, aren't you?"

"No," he said, without the faintest wince or smile. "Not that. It was a serious question."

"Of course I feel like that," she said. "Doesn't everyone? Well, maybe you don't, given that you have such a nice suit, which probably means that you have a nice car and a nice house and a nice family and a nice tax accountant, but everyone who lives in this place does. It's what they call a sink estate—the kind the council has difficulty filling. Not that I'm ungrateful, you understand; if it wasn't for places that nobody wants to live, unattached and childless people like me wouldn't have a cat in hell's chance of getting to the head of the housing queue."

"But with you the feeling's more profound," he said, intoning it as a statement rather than a question. "Whatever they feel, most of the people living here are perfectly understandable products of their environment, and most have adapted to it as well as they can. They may not like it, but they fit in. They mostly don't have jobs, but they do have careers of a kind. They have their social circles, and they have their children. You don't. You can't hold on to any social relationships for long, and you can't conceive. You have difficulty sleeping at night and alcohol doesn't even make you drunk, let alone happy, because you get sick before you get high."

Frankie could have complained about one or two of the brushstrokes, but the big picture was devastatingly accurate. "What exactly are you selling?" she asked, coldly. The sales pitch was far too near the knuckle and she couldn't figure out how or why she'd been targeted, given that the social relationships she could never hold on to for long included any and all jobs, thus rendering her purse as impotent as her screwed-up womb.

"You're a changeling, Miss Harrap," he said, baldly. "You really don't fit in here. You're not even human." His manner was still perfectly amiable, and he didn't seem to be conscious of the fact that he was saying dreadful things.

He means it, she thought. *He really does.*

"That's funny," she said. "The doctors didn't notice anything out of place when they took my genetic fingerprint a while ago."

He condescended to raise an eyebrow at that.

"It's all the rage around here," she added, sarcastically. "Every time there's a rape or a messy murder down at ground zero, the police appeal for volunteers so that the innocent can be eliminated from their enquiries. It's the one respect in which this humble architectural carbuncle is right on the cutting edge of social progress. One day, everybody will be gene-mapped at birth, so that all rapists can be instantly identified. Anyone who's not human will show up as well, of course."

"No they won't," the man said, quietly. "We can get around problems like that. The greater part of your body is engineered to *seem* human even at the biochemical level, but the greater part of your body isn't really *you* at all. The real you is inside your head, Miss Harrap; what you're walking around in is just a disguise."

She thought about that for a minute or two. It was difficult to believe that he was any ordinary kind of lunatic, given his gear, but she still couldn't see the point of his spinning her a line. What on earth did he hope to gain?

"What you're saying," she said, "is that I'm a little lost alien. Not so much *ET*, more like *Invasion of the Body-Snatchers*. I'm a pod, and the reason I've had such a shitty life is that I don't know I'm a pod and never figured out how to get together with all the other pods."

"That's exactly right," he said. "I know that you can't quite believe it yet, but it *is* true. Your superior intelligence and mental flexibility drew you to the correct conclusion like a magnet. All you have to do now is accept it. That's why I'm here."

"You're a pod too, I suppose?" she said. "An alien invader—part of a secret army from some other star-system, come to conquer earth. I saw the movie—in fact, I saw all twenty movies."

"You'll find it easier to understand if you can take aboard the ideas without the paranoia," he told her, without sounding as if he were ticking her off. "Yes, we're from another star-system. Yes, for the sake of being able to live among mankind we disguise ourselves as human beings—but our real purpose is to observe without our presence as observers affecting the phenomena under observation. We're not soldiers, we're anthropologists."

Frankie drained the dregs from her mug and set it down on the side-table. *At least it's not boring*, she thought. *If it turns out to be a clever sales pitch now, I'll be quite disappointed.*

"How, exactly, do you insert your agents into human society?" she asked, trying to match his benign politeness. "Why don't I remember being sent forth on my mission to observe?"

"Participant observation is a delicate business," the alien told her, blandly. "It can go badly awry if the people under observation know they're being observed, but it can also produce poor results if the observers don't become fully cognizant of the customs and folkways of those they're observing. Our method—and we don't claim it's perfect, merely that it's the best available—is to use changelings. We substitute our agents for human babies within a few hours of birth. Our agents aren't infants themselves, but their higher mind functions are suppressed, and they aren't self-conscious. As the changeling is reared by its foster-parents it develops as if it were a normal human infant, but at a strategic moment—usually at the on-set of adolescence—we make contact with the agent and induce him or her to drink *this*."

From an inner pocket of his jacket the man produced a small glass vial full of viscous pink liquid. It looked rather like a miniature strawberry milk shake.

"And what does that do?" Frankie asked.

"It begins the awakening progress by which the agent regains full consciousness of his or her nature and previous experience. This recovered self-consciousness is superimposed on the human-imitative host self-consciousness that the growing pseudohuman has developed, who therefore becomes a kind of mental hybrid, able to move within human society and able to interpret what goes on there while simultaneously remaining detached from it. It isn't true objec-tivity, but it's the next best thing, methodologically speaking. You do understand all this, don't you?"

"Oh yes," Frankie said. "I did Sociology A level once, at the tech. I had some crazy idea about training to be a social worker—helping other people with backgrounds and problems as bad as mine. I didn't stick it, of course, but the sociology was interesting, in a bizarre sort of way. But that was a long time ago, as I'm sure you'll appreciate. I'm a long, long way past puberty, Mr. Pod."

"I know," he said. "We...lost you. It wasn't easy to find you, in the circumstances."

A terrible suspicion began to dawn on Frankie. "You mean...," she began.

"I mean that the person charged with the job of making the ex-change of babies somehow made a mess of it," he said. "As you can imagine, it's not easy switching babies within twenty-four hours of birth, and we certainly don't like to be caught doing it. We're usu-ally very careful, but somehow, you were switched for the wrong baby. We keep the babies we take for research purposes for a few weeks, before putting them back into human society *via* adoption agencies, but a couple of weeks went by before we did a gene-analysis of the baby we ended up with, and realized that it wasn't the one we'd intended to take. We'd intended to place you with a Mr. and Mrs. Howarth—pleasant and prosperous people who'd be able to give you a stable home with all the advantages—whom we'd researched very thoroughly, as we always do. Instead, it seems, we gave you to two travelers who'd only paused in Naburn so that your mother could give birth.

"When we tried to find you, it was already too late. The parents gave a false name at the hospital, probably because the father—assuming that the man your mother was with was the father—had jumped bail and didn't want the police to find him. They didn't register the birth, and took good care to vanish. There aren't very many of us in this part of the world—or, indeed, in the world as a whole—but we did try to track you down. We never actually stopped trying, in fact, but after a while...well, it began to seem like an impossible task."

"Yes," Frankie said, remembering what it had been like when she was very young. "It seemed that way to me, too, when I eventually started trying to find out who I really was. The last set of foster-parents I was placed with were quite helpful, but neither they nor the social services had anything to go on—no record at all before the age of six. My mother didn't tell them anything substantial when she handed me in, and without a birth-certificate there was no place to start. I did have a few scraps of information, though...and a few memories. It took a long time and a lot of looking, but in the end I managed to find some other travelers who'd known my mum, and they were able to point me in the right direction. I found out that I was born in Naburn, and when. Then...."

"If you hadn't started making your own enquiries," the bland man interrupted, irritatingly, "we probably wouldn't have been able to start ours again. If you hadn't gone there...did they tell you that other people had enquired about you?" He was still holding the vial in his hand, in an oddly reverent fashion, patiently waiting for the moment when she might feel able to take it.

"Yes," Frankie murmured. "They certainly did. But I don't think...."

"I'm truly sorry," he said. "It was an unforgivable mistake, but we'll do everything in our power to put things right. When you drink this, things will begin to be set right. Believe me, you won't regret it. I know you've been laboring under the misapprehension that you're human for far too long, and it's only natural that you'll be scared, but it will make things far, far better. Once you've drunk this, and begun to awake from your long nightmare, your life will turn around completely. From now on, things will be better than you ever imagined possible. I suppose you find all this utterly incredible, but that doesn't matter; you only have to drink this down and the truth of everything I've told you will begin to become manifest."

The funny thing was that she did believe him. She believed every word. If things had been different, she'd have taken it for granted that he was out of his mind, but the fact that he plainly didn't know the whole truth made it so much easier to believe that the partial truth he did know was indeed true.

"If I had a gun in the house," Frankie said, bleakly, "I'd blow your fucking brains out. I really would. For two pins I'd go to the kitchen and take out my one sharp knife and hack you bloodily to bits, and I wouldn't give a tinker's fuck about the fact that the police would never believe that I was only stamping on some lousy alien bug."

"Please, Miss Harrap," said the alien anthropologist mildly. "Just drink it down. Then we can begin all over again. Everything will be all right, now."

"You stupid bastard," Frankie said, wishing that she could put more feeling into the insult. "You stupid, incompetent, alien bastard. I'm not the person you think I am. I'm not the real Frances Harrap."

The carefully-faked man was clearly incapable of genuine astonishment or honest alarm, but at least he had the grace to look thoroughly puzzled.

"The Frances Harrap you're looking for," she told him, wearily, "is dead. Her name was Julie Ann Howarth, and she went to stand on a train line, in front of an oncoming inter-city 125, two weeks after she found out who she really was...or who I really was...except that you...oh, fuck it. It wasn't your agent who took the wrong baby, you moron—the nurse had already mixed us up."

The alien simply looked blank, as if his computer-like brain was having trouble coming to terms with this news.

"When I went to the hospital," Frankie told him, wearily, "they told me that the Howarths had been trying to find me for years. They didn't mention anyone else—I suppose your people avoided giving them any explanation and the hospital administrators just assumed that all the enquirers were connected. The Howarths found out that Julie Ann wasn't their real daughter when she had to have a blood transfusion after a road accident. At first they tried to ignore the fact, but simple curiosity about the whereabouts of their own flesh-and-blood gradually got the better of them. They tried to conceal what they were doing from Julie Ann, but that just made things worse. She was well on the way to deep unhappiness before I came along and the whole sorry story...or what we all thought was the whole sorry story...came out. That's why I had the tests done on my own

DNA—to confirm that I really was the Howarths' daughter. Except that once they'd met me, and found out what my life had been like...suddenly, they weren't so very interested in a glorious reunion. After all, it's not as if I'm *pretty*, is it.

"Meanwhile, your missing anthropologist killed herself, for all the reasons you sketched out to me a few minutes ago...and one or two extra ones besides. It was all a bit of a bummer for me too, as you might be able to imagine if you were human. The mix-up seems to fucked us all up, one way or another."

The anthropologist was still blank and uncomprehending. He seemed to be a bit slow on the uptake for an alien mastermind.

"Your changeling was where you intended her to be all along, you idiot," Frankie said, spelling it out. "You only thought you'd got it wrong because you got the wrong baby in exchange. If what you've told me is really the truth, you could have given Julie Ann the drink on her thirteenth birthday and she'd have been just fine."

"But we thought....," he began, floundering in the sticky depths of his discovered misconceptions.

"You thought wrong," Frankie informed him. "Your human disguises are a little too perfect. You can't even penetrate them yourselves unless you know for sure."

"Are you sure...?" he began.

It was her turn to interrupt, confident in the superiority of her own wisdom. "Your pseudohuman bodies are supposed to be sterile, right?" Frankie said, angrily. "You told me I couldn't conceive when you were listing the symptoms of my existential malaise with such deadly accuracy."

"Yes," he said.

"Well I can't, *now*," she said. "But the reason I can't is that I had three fucking abortions in my teens and one of them was botched. I'm a self-made disaster, Mr. Pod. I'm alien through and through, and maybe that is because I was a changeling, switched at birth, but it has nothing whatsoever to do with you, and there's not a damn thing in all the world that your precious elixir can do for *me*. Have you got that through your thick pseudohuman skull yet?"

He had. He looked at her very calmly, in full and obvious possession of his faculties. He carefully put the vial back in the inside pocket of his jacket. "You do realize," he said, dully, "that if you tell anyone the story I've just told you, they won't believe you. They'll think you're mad."

"They wouldn't be far wrong," Frankie assured him.

The unexpected visitor stood up, wriggled in his suit so it sat properly upon his shoulders, and went to the door. "Don't get up," he said, without the least trace of irony. "I'll see myself out."

"You'll never get down those stairs in one piece," she told him. "The local kids'll be queuing up for first crack at you, Stanley knives at the ready."

"I'll be all right," he assured her, with perfect confidence. "I'm usually very competent, you know—I don't make many mistakes."

"Maybe not," she conceded, ungraciously. "After all, it's not as if you're only human, is it?"

She heard the outer door close as he went out. He didn't slam it. She wondered if it would have been better or worse if he'd turned out to be a con man, a rapist or a Scientologist. He had, at any rate, been far more plausible than a Mormon or a Jehovah's Witness. She wondered, too, if it would really have been so much better if she *had* been an alien anthropologist accidentally mislaid by her fellows, or whether it would really have been so much better if the Howarths hadn't been so utterly appalled to find out what had become of their flesh-and-blood daughter after five years on the road with the travelers and a further ten in assorted children's homes and foster-homes.

Surely it wasn't such an ill wind that everybody has to be counted as losers, she thought. Surely Julie Ann could have given herself a break and counted her blessings. Surely I'm no worse off than I was before simply because I know what I missed out on. Surely....

She went into the bedroom, and sat down once again at the dressing-table. She turned round and reached out to take the pen from where it had fallen near the head of the bed. It had left a big black stain on the crumpled sheet.

On the mockingly blank sheet of paper, she wrote: EARTH HAS BEEN INVADED BY ALIEN AN-THROPOLOGISTS. After a pause, she added: BUT DON'T WORRY TOO MUCH ABOUT IT, BECAUSE THEY'RE A RIGHT LOAD OF PILLOCKS.

She threw the pen over her shoulder, harder than before. It hit the wall and fell on to the floor on the far side of the bed. Then she took the brandy bottle in her right hand and a handful of pills in her left.

She took a swig of Armagnac, then set the bottle down again. She sat still for half a minute, waiting. She wasn't thinking about anything in particular—she was too numb for that.

In the end, though, her mind simply wouldn't stay blank.

I wonder what the alien anthropologists will make of us when they have to write it all up, she thought. What will they make of the saintly, sane and sanitized Howarths, and the unsaintly, insane, un-sanitary Harraps? How will they explain it all? How can they even begin to understand? Will their readers be able to believe it, or will they think it's all just a silly travelers' tale?

She got up, walked over to the window, opened it, and threw out the handful of pills. She watched them fall thirteen floors to the ground.

It would have been appropriate, in a way, had they fallen on Mr. Pod's head, but he was nowhere to be seen. It was as if he'd vanished into thin air.

She fetched the cereal-bowl and emptied every last pill out of the window. It was a reckless thing to do—after all, there were people living not a million miles away who'd have given her a good few quid for the tranks and the anti-depressants—but she was in a reckless mood.

She went back to the dressing-table, screwed up the bit of paper, and threw it in the corner, where there ought to have been a waste-paper bin. Then she went back into the living-room and started scanning the rows of books, thinking that perhaps, after all, it had been really stupid to think about killing herself when she hadn't even read them all yet. She knew that she'd have to live for a whole week on tea and brandy, until her next giro arrived, but that wasn't so terrible a prospect, given that she'd been meaning to go on a diet for months.

"Suicide might be the only way out if I were Julie Ann Howarth, *alias* the real Frances Harrap, *alias* the Body Snatcher from Outer Space," Frankie said, not caring at all about the awful incongruity of talking to an empty room, "but I'm not. It's not what I've been, or could have been, or ought to have been that matters. I shouldn't need a miniature strawberry milkshake to help me to be *me*. I ought to be able to do that on my own, and I bloody well will."

And then, proudly, she burst into tears.

COMING TO TERMS
WITH THE GREAT PLAGUE

IT DIDN'T HELP that the doctor's waiting-room was plastered with posters exhorting all and sundry to

CHECK YOUR MEMORIES REGULARLY

Others paraded dozens of mug-shots beneath the accusing legend:

DO YOU "REMEMBER" ANY OF THESE PEOPLE?

Marilyn was there, of course, third from the left on the second bottom row. I've always thought of myself as a hard-headed sort of person, but I couldn't help feeling that they were trying to steal her away from me. Nor could I help hoping, even though I knew full well that the hope was absurd, that in this one instance—and only this one instance—they were quite mistaken about the fact of her non-existence.

It could be worse, I told myself, sternly, as my name was called over the tannoy. *It would be worse if they actually did exist— especially for them. The problems that arise for all the people who remember Marilyn are trivial compared with the problems a real Marilyn would face as a result of being remembered.*

Dr. Vernon took one look at me and said, in world-weary fashion: "What's the trouble, Mr. Hayling? FMS?"

I blushed. I knew that the tabloids had taken to calling the FMS plague a pandemic, but he surely had to play host to the usual crop of throat infections, arthritic joints and suspicious lumps as well. I gave him the benefit of the doubt and assumed that I must look too robustly healthy for it to be anything else.

"Which one?" he asked, in response to the tiniest of nods. I'd been hoping to lead up to it a little more gently than that. I couldn't produce her name in the blunt and businesslike fashion which

22

seemed to be required of me; even though I knew full well what she was, it would have been a kind of betrayal. False or not, the memories were good. We'd been so happy together, and it really hadn't been her fault that we'd broken up. To dismiss her, utterly without ceremony, as the product of a mysterious rogue infection might be necessary, but it still seemed rather a shabby thing to do.

"It's all right," he said, impatiently. "I'm a doctor. I'm not going to tell anyone else, and I'm certainly not going to attack you in a fit of unreasoning jealousy. Believe me, Mr. Hayling, I've had a lot of experience dealing with FMS. By now, every doctor in the developed world is an old hand."

I managed to stutter an M sound three or four times.

"Marilyn," he said. I didn't dare ask whether it was a fifty-fifty guess, or whether Marilyn was significantly more common in the Thames Valley than Melanie, or whether there was some particular quirk that marked me as a Marilyn type. The tabloids were quick to pounce on the least rumor about patterns in the data, but they'd cried wolf so often that the man in the street wouldn't stand a chance of identifying an authentic discovery in the chaos of speculation. There had to be some real patterns in the data—if there weren't, what was the point in people reporting the details to their doctors?—although there hadn't been the slightest whisper about any effective treatment or possible cure.

Dr. Vernon called up a data-sheet that was already marked up with questions and boxes, so that he could map my condition with a few deft clicks of his mouse. He was able to fill in a lot of the boxes at one fell swoop, simply by transferring information from my file. "To what time-period do the memories relate?" he asked, wincing at his own clumsy phraseology.

"Thirteen to fifteen years ago," I said. "I might never have figured out that they weren't the real thing if her face hadn't kept coming up on the TV and posters like the one in your waiting-room. I met her...that is, I remember meeting her...shortly after starting work with VirtIconics in July 1993. She moved in with me after three months, and moved out again a year after that. I heard from her—I remember hearing from her—half a dozen times more, although I only saw her in the flesh once." *Oh, the delicious pain of that meeting! The regrets, the tears, the sense of tragedy!* I coughed to cover my sudden discomfiture and hastened on. "There's nothing at all after I first met Jill in '96...that's my wife. She's real enough. She has to be—she works for a solicitor."

He didn't bother to contrive a polite grin to acknowledge the attempted witticism.

"Do you have any objective record of your movements between 1993 and 1996?" he asked.

"No. Who does? Who knew we were going to need them, way back then?"

"Not even a business diary with a record of appointments? A Sasco—something like that?"

I shook my head. I'd kept my appointments on a Stone Age personal organizer with no hard disc and I'd thrown my Sascos in the bin every new year, like any sane person.

"Are there any evident anomalies in the Marilyn memory-pattern, or is it entirely consistent with your other memories of the period?"

"Sometimes I can get flashes of living alone during '94, but I can't seem to get a grip on them; the false memories seem to have overlain and obliterated the true ones very efficiently. There is one thing, though...." I hesitated. No sooner had I managed to slip into clinical/objective mode than I'd been jerked right out of it again by a rush of resentment at the thought that all this was private, too intimately personal to be discussed with some quack who'd never understand in a million years what Marilyn and I had meant to one another.

"Please go on," he said. "Information about anomalies is vital to our attempt to comprehend the FMS phenomenon."

"It may not mean anything. It's just that...well, everybody calls me Jack these days, but that's because I'm married to Jill. Before we became an item I was always John to everyone...but Marilyn called me Jack. It's not inconsistent, as such...I guess people who get close to one another often use names that are different, their special prerogative...but Jack came from Jill, you see...it's probably nothing."

"I wouldn't say so," said Dr. Vernon, showing a flicker of real interest for the first time. "It's actually rather interesting. Even if it's simply evidence of incompetence on the part of the agent, that kind of detail might help to tell us something about the way the agent plunders your real memories in order to construct the false ones. It's also possible that it's something your own mind did, subconsciously—planting a booby-trap, as it were, to tip off the conscious mind that something is amiss with the memory-pattern. If people are able to draw on the resources of some kind of psychological immune-system to cancel out the agent's effects there might be hope of recovery even while we haven't yet identified the agent or devised any kind of biochemical treatment."

He accompanied the final statement with what was presumably intended to be a morale-boosting smile. Doctors and biotechnologists always referred to *the agent*, even though there wasn't the faintest trace, so far, of any physical cause for the false memories that were spring up here, there and everywhere. It wasn't just a matter of needing a label—it was a bid for property rights, an insistence that the syndrome was *their* problem, not something that could any longer be left to therapists and other assorted charlatans.

"Can you make a reliable estimate of the time of origin of the false memories?" Dr. Vernon asked, in a carefully elliptical fashion.

"They can't have been in place very long," I said, "or I'd have recognized the face in the TV ads when they first began broadcasting it. I guess the memories crept up on me, so I can't be absolutely sure, but it was about last Tuesday when I began thinking that the Marilyn they kept showing with the FMS updates was uncannily like *my* Marilyn, and how awful it would be if *she* turned out to be...well, I guess you know how it goes. I'd say the infection is about ten days to a fortnight old."

"That's good. The sooner these things are spotted, the sooner you can start to work against them. Have you made a preliminary record of the memory-complex yet?"

"It's not finished," I lied. I knew I had to use it, but I wasn't about to go public with it, no matter how useful it might be as a research tool. He didn't seem surprised by my answer and he didn't press the point.

"Just make sure it's as full as you can make it," he said. "Unless you record everything you can presently remember, you won't be able to track the extension of the pattern. Not that it's certain to grow, mind—at the moment it looks like a relatively low-level invasion, not too ambitious and conveniently distant, and it might well stay that way." He didn't sound optimistic. The smile looked as if it might fall off at any moment and the fingers of his left hand were fidgeting with the mouse in a fashion which seemed almost feverish.

"I'll get on to it," I assured him. "If I find any more anomalies, I'll be sure to let you know."

"Have you told your wife what's happening?"

"Not yet."

His expression was more sorrowful than disapproving. "In my experience," he said, "it's better to do it sooner than later. She'll catch on soon enough—the time you put into record-keeping will give you away eventually, even if there are no other signs. It's probable that she'll be unable to avoid some feeling of jealousy, even if she accepts on a conscious and rational level that you can't help what's happening to you. Some women, paradoxical as it may seem,

25

think that their partners starting to remember non-existent women is even worse than their actually being unfaithful."

"Jill's not like that," I told him, wishing that I could be certain. "She'll understand." I was sure that she'd try. Unfortunately, nobody understood why the FMS plague was happening at all, let alone why the false memories suffered by men were almost invariably memories of hot love affairs with beautiful women, while the false memories suffered by women were usually memories of children they'd never actually borne. So far, Jill had shown no sign of any of those, despite the fact that she and I were childless...or if she had, she'd kept them entirely to herself.

"I'll need to take a blood sample," the doctor said, reaching into a desk-drawer for a hypodermic. "Part of it will be inspected; the rest will be frozen, so that it can be screened retrospectively for any candidate agents thrown up by future research."

"The only problem with that," I pointed out, to show that I was a scientifically-sophisticated person who was on the ball, "will be finding a reliable control group so you can check for the candidate-agent's absence." Anyone with a grain of common sense could see that for every person who managed to figure out that they were playing host to false memories there could easily be two or three who couldn't, and two or three more who wouldn't admit it even if they could. Ever skeptical of the competence and motives of my fellow human beings, I had a sneaking suspicion that by the time some hero identified a virus or a psychotropic molecule that might be responsible for the plague, they might not be able to find a single unexposed person this side of the arctic circle.

Dr. Vernon, who was presumably a realist himself, contented himself with a somber nod as he carefully fitted the needle to the plastic syringe. I reflected on the painful irony of the fact that although there were a dozen different ways of getting things into the body nowadays, there was still only one effective method of taking blood out.

* * * * * * *

I WASN'T PARTICULARLY late getting to the office, and I was well into flexitime credit, but I couldn't help feeling a paranoid suspicion that people were looking at me—that they'd somehow guessed where I'd been and what I'd confessed to the doctor. It was silly, but I was all too well aware of the ways in which FMS sufferers could accidentally give themselves away, and of the awful rapacity of office gossip. Nobody bothered speculating any more about people's *real* affairs—in fact, I sometimes wonder whether, in these troubled times, people actually bother having real affairs any more.

There was nothing in the least unusual in the fact that as soon as five of us had gathered around a table in the Turk's Head at lunch-time—variously clutching our BLT toasties, pizza wedges, baked potatoes and pints—the conversation should instantly turn to FMS. Even so, I couldn't help feeling horribly uncomfortable about it. I couldn't help wondering which of the others might be feeling the same, and whether any of them might secretly be harboring fond memories of passionate frolics with *my* Marilyn—and I couldn't help suspecting that every single word that was spoken was aimed directly at me, was really about me.

"If you see FMS in its proper historical perspective," Mike Gilbert said, as his bushy black beard gradually filled up with crumbs, "it's bloody obvious what it is. It's psychological warfare, that's what. I mean, where did it start? All those bloody therapists uncovering repressed memories of sexual abuse suffered in childhood, setting generation against generation, sibling against sibling. The purpose had to be disruption and destabilization of the entire social structure—and when people figured out that the memories were false the psychowarriors promptly moved on to something more insidious. Every day you hear reports of men killing one another in jealous rages over women who never even existed, but that's just the tip of the iceberg...the real disruption is inside, in the way people look at one another suspiciously, saying nothing, just wondering. The entire fabric of Western society is coming apart, stitch by stitch."

Ouch! I thought.

"Who's doing it, then?" Hal Mellor scoffed, after taking another gluttonous swig from a glass that was already almost empty. "The ex-communists? The Pacific Rimmers? The green zealots?"

"Mike's right," Aileen McMurdo put in, in that deadly earnest tone she only ever used when she was taking the piss. "You have to see it in its true historical context. It actually started before the child abuse revelations, with all those stories about people being kidnapped aboard UFOs and subjected to intensive examination by aliens. That's the key to the mystery."

"That didn't destabilize anything," Hal pointed out. "Who'd start a war in a crazy way like that?"

"The aliens would," Aileen came back, springing the trap. "It was all double bluff, see. They planted lots of false memories of abduction to make sure that the people who'd really been abducted wouldn't be believed—and what they found out from all those tests

27

was how to screw up our minds utterly and completely. They found out how to refine their weapons for maximum effect on human beings, and now they're using the second-generation stuff. By the time the invasion fleet gets here we'll all be psychological wrecks, every vestige of our real pasts consumed by obsessive nostalgia for lost lovers and dead babies. We won't offer a whimper of resistance—in fact, we'll probably be queuing up to be first into the gas chambers."

"Did you make that one up all by yourself?" Mike asked, in a mock-admiring tone which was something of a double bluff itself.

"No, she didn't," said Helen Chambers, who spent far too much time exchanging intricate jokes with Aileen for her own good. "She's being paid to put it about. She's an *agent provocateur* for the real masterminds."

"Who are?" I put in. I had to play my part, lest my silence should become suspicious.

"Don't pretend you don't know, Jack," she said, with a broad and exceedingly discomfiting wink. "We're all friends here. We all know who it really is, even though we've all been sworn to secrecy."

"No harm in telling us, then, is there?" I countered.

"Well, it's us, isn't it?" she said. "VirtIconics, traders in synthetic reality. It's the market research department testing the water, trying to figure out what kinds of virtual reality will sell best...and maybe breaking down consumer resistance a little. After all, what's the ideal consumer profile for buyers of high-powered virtual reality hardware? People whose grip on reality is so weak that they can't even trust their own memories. We humble designers of machine-generated dreams are merely cogs in a much vaster system, whose ambition to extend the limits of human experience is literally unlimited."

"You want to be careful, Helen," Aileen said. "At least one of these guys must be a spy for the suits upstairs. They'll be down on you like a ton of bricks if they find out you've been giving away the company's darkest secrets. Anyway, it can't be the marketing department—they wouldn't bother with trivia like sexual passion and mother love if they could get down to the real nitty-gritty of product placement. If they really had FMS down to fine art and crude technology those warning broadcasts would be full of pictures of canned beers and drain-cleaners and laser-discs that aren't available in any video-stores. What kind of a world do you think we're living in, for God's sake?"

"This is getting silly," Mike observed, affably. He was probably feeling pleased because he'd kicked the whole thing off, or maybe because Hal's patience had run out and he was bringing back a second round of drinks before anyone else had finished their first.

"Except, of course," Hal said, as he plonked the glasses down on the crowded tabletop, "that if they ever do find the cause, it could stop being a plague and start being a technology. If it *isn't* us, it could end up being the competition that will wipe us out. We could end up taking our VR products into a marketplace where we'd have to compete with people selling designer memories. Can you see the ads? ALL THE HOLIDAYS OF A LIFETIME...THE PAST IS A THOUSAND FOREIGN COUNTRIES...WHATEVER YOU WANT, YOU CAN REMEMBER...MEMORIES ARE MADE OF...hell, this really isn't very funny, is it? We could be left high and dry, showing off our Sopwith Camels the day after someone else invented the supersonic jet."

"And it wouldn't just be one lifetime," I said, judiciously striking the same note of fake anxiety just in case any real anxiety happened to show through. "Like Mike and Aileen said, we have to remember the historical context. Before the child abuse there were the aliens, and before the aliens there were the past lives, when everybody was finding out that they'd been Napoleon or Cleopatra in a former incarnation. That can't have been *our* marketing department, unless all *our* memories are false. IBM maybe, or AT&T, but definitely not us."

"Forget marketing," Aileen said. "The bozos up there don't have the imagination. It's definitely aliens. That reincarnation stuff was just more of their disinformation. Of course, they might not be planning to invade at all. They might actually be benign, intent on helping us to fulfill our true evolutionary potential. Maybe the whole FMS saga is just a series of psychological adaptations, which will culminate when we've finally been pressured into becoming true masters of memory, able to take mature responsibility for the reconstruction of our personalities, fit for membership of the galactic community."

"Oh, sure," said Helen, who was never particularly squeamish about hitting below the belt when she was lashing out at random. "The way these guys keep inventing women that never existed to compensate for their failures with real women, and then get into fights about who the imaginary women really liked best, is a giant leap forward for mankind. We're well on the way to true maturity now, aren't we?"

It was a step too far. I bit my lip, but Hal—who'd put away his second pint in double-quick time—didn't. "Exactly what made you so sour about men, Helen?" he asked, before he could stop himself. "Some guy leave you holding a baby boy that died, or what?"

That killed the conversation stone dead—and made me wonder exactly what, and exactly who, was accelerating Hal's drinking problem.

* * * * * * *

BY THE TIME I got home I'd decided to make a clean breast of things, but I had to wait for the right moment—you can't just blurt these things out as you cross the threshold when you know perfectly well that you've both had an absolutely bloody day at the office. Jill was as whacked as I was. If it hadn't been for a strong desire to keep things as normal as possible I'd have volunteered to cook, even though it was her turn.

By the time we were fed and suitably relaxed the weary temptation stole upon me to leave it for another day, but I knew it wasn't a good idea. The bullet had to be bitten, and if she hadn't noticed already that something was amiss she soon would.

"I had to pop in to see the doctor on my way to work this morning," I told her, tentatively, while we'd both collapsed on the couch in front of the TV. It was showing a soap opera, one of whose chief characters was just beginning to get to grips with the legacy of his intense imaginary involvement with an entirely fictitious Veronica. I steeled myself against the anticipated look of alarm.

She did turn her grey-green eyes full on me, but there was more reproach in the gaze than alarm.

"I thought something was up," she murmured, sadly. "I suppose it had to come."

"It's not serious," I hastened to tell her. "Dr. Vernon confirmed that. Distant past, short duration. Hardly anything, really."

"But it could get worse, couldn't it?" she said. "There's no knowing how far it will go. You hear stories about people reconstructing their entire pasts from day one, losing themselves entirely."

"That's very rare," I told her. "The tabloids exaggerate. One in ten Britons are suffering from the syndrome, but life goes on. The country hasn't ground to a halt. Personally, I think the epidemic's losing its force. They do, you know. Even the most devastating diseases weaken over time. We may not have an effective treatment yet but the simple fact that we know about it and are on our guard makes a big difference. It's much harder for the false memories to take hold and spread now we can recognize them for what they are.

I'm keeping proper records, and I'll do the checks every day. I'm fighting it, Jill, and if determination is enough to win, I'll beat it."

I had begun to babble, and would have rambled on, but she cut me short. "It's a girl, isn't it," she said. She was trying to keep her voice level, but I could hear the sense of injury, the dark fear that she was being crowded out of my past by someone younger and more beautiful.

"It's just the form the disease usually takes," I told her, taking her hand in mine and caressing it with all the reassurance I could muster. "It doesn't *mean* anything."

She didn't pull her hand away but I could feel the tension in the muscles. "That's what they all say," she said. "*It doesn't mean anything. I can't help it. It's just a stray virus. It could happen to any*one. All very convenient, isn't it? You don't have to do anything, except lie back and enjoy it. You don't have to take responsibility for the fact that your innermost soul is being colonized by some little whore who's doing the same for ten per cent of the fucking population."

She wasn't babbling, and she wasn't angry. Indeed, she was frighteningly articulate. Actually, less than five per cent of the population had the form of FMS involving female lovers and less than five per cent of that five per cent had the form involving Marilyn, but it was no time to be pedantic.

"It *is* a disease," I said, feebly. "It really is." There were, of course, some people who argued that it wasn't, that the spread of the syndrome was due to the power of auto-suggestion aided and abetted by the media—the modern day equivalent of absent-mindedly scanning a few pages of a medical encyclopedia and convincing yourself that you have everything from asthma to bilharzia. They even had a jargon for it, borrowed from the sociobiologists. According to them, Marilyn and all her sisters were just memes: infectious ideas designed by natural selection to survive and thrive. If they were right, the soap opera whose signature tune was filling the living-room was taking a big risk. The fictitious Veronica might suddenly start cropping up in the memories of millions of couch potatoes. Maybe the plot-line was an experiment, designed to discover whether such a thing could happen. Wouldn't that add some spice to the tired old debates about the psychological effects of media sex and violence?

"I know," Jill said, trying hard to make it sound sincere, although her fist was still half-clenched. "I know it's just a disease really. I'm sorry."

"It hasn't affected *you*, love," I told her. "The fake memories have only colonized the time before I met you. They won't *displace* you. They can't. You're far too important to me." The promises were reckless—no matter how much confidence I had in my own hard-headedness and self-possession I really wasn't in a position to offer any guarantees—but I had to make them anyway.

"Why not?" she countered, dispiritedly. "You and I live in the real world, and always have done. We always had to cope with the bloody-mindedness of chance and change. The narrative of our relationship couldn't skip the boring bits and all our conversations had to be *ad-libbed*. Your new old relationship doesn't labor under those handicaps, does it? It has all the advantages of unreality."

It would hardly have been diplomatic to assure her that it really didn't seem that way—that my memories of Marilyn were just as full of awkwardness and mischance as any real relationship could and would have been—so I cast about for a safer line of thought.

"I'm afraid you'll have to show a little extra vigilance from now on," I said, stroking her wrist and forearm with assiduous gentleness. "If this thing is contagious you're bound to be in danger of picking it up from me."

"I suppose you'd like that," she said, bitterly. "It would let you off the hook, wouldn't it? And it wouldn't bother you the way it bothers me, because I probably wouldn't be remembering some muscular super-stud hung like a horse—it's odds-on that I'd just be remembering a baby I never had. Well, that wouldn't be so bad for me, either, given that I never did have any babies because of your green conscience. Unfortunately, like everything else in life, the syndrome seems by all accounts to be utterly perverse. It's mostly slags who've already had two or three kids in defiance of all the propaganda who are remembering extra ones, while the barren heroines like me are stubbornly immune."

That wasn't fair. The issue of children had been fully discussed. It had been a mutual decision. Anyway, rumor had it that the female version of FMS could be just as discomfiting as the male version often was, if not more so. Some of the remembered death scenes were said to be harrowing enough to drive their victims into deep melancholia. At least the phantom women mostly contented themselves with Dear John faxes or phone calls. No one knew how many lives the plague had so far claimed, but female suicides encouraged by ersatz grief probably outnumbered male murders instigated by unreasoning jealous rages.

While I was still contemplating the unfairness of her latest argumentative move, Jill seized the conversational initiative. "Which one is she?" she asked.

I wanted to say that it didn't matter—because, of course, it really didn't—but I daren't. She would have been deeply suspicious of my motives; it would only have increased her anxiety.

"Marilyn," I said, baldly.

"The stringy blonde with the snub nose? Christ, Jack, I didn't know you liked the *gamine* type."

"I didn't *choose* her, Jill."

"No, but you're collaborating with it, aren't you? Subconsciously if not consciously. You have to be. What else could determine the multiple forms the syndrome takes?"

"There's no way out of that, is there?" I said, miserably. "My subconscious has to carry the can for whatever my consciousness denies. It's Catch-22 all over again. Nobody knows, love. Nobody knows why the syndrome takes the forms it does—and nobody really knows how many forms it can take. The girls are easy enough to identify, and the extra babies, but how can we tell how many fakes there are which just slip unobtrusively into the patterns of people's pasts, creating no anomalies and arousing no suspicions? There might be millions of people who think they're clear purely and simply because they haven't any way of identifying the lies that have crept into their lives."

I didn't intend that the remarks should be taken personally—but that, inevitably, was the way she took them.

"I suppose you think I don't even have the imagination to dream up a dead baby," she said. "After all, you're the big shot software engineer working at the cutting edge of masturbation technology at good old VirtIconics, and I'm just a common-or-garden office hack working for a bunch of shysters. You breathe, eat and dream virtual realities while I itemize grounds for divorce and type up wills. I've never once been sexually abused by my father or taken aboard a flying saucer for a smear test. All I can remember is school and college and *you*. Maybe you're the fake. Maybe you always have been. How could I tell?"

She didn't mean any of it, and in the end it got on top of her. By the time she was half way through the speech she was punctuating the sentences with choked sobs, and by the time she reached the last full stop she was weeping. I let go of her wrist and put my arms around her, nestling her head on my shoulder and hugging her tight.

Actions speak louder than words, and she took far more comfort from my silence than she'd been able to wring out of my awkward, stumbling words. I took comfort from it too; she was warm and damp and vulnerable, and I felt that I wanted to hold her forever...but I couldn't help remembering that once upon a time I'd felt exactly the same about poor, frail Marilyn when I'd hugged her in just that tender and loving way.

Nothing lasts, I thought. Nothing endures. *It isn't just our names that are writ in water, Mr. Keats.*

* * * * * * *

I COULDN'T STAY with Jill for more than an hour, even though I felt she needed me. I had work to do. I had to check the hard copy of my affair with Marilyn, which I'd made surreptitiously over the weekend, to make sure that no new details were piling up in the storeroom of my memory. I also had to file an account of my movements on the hard disc of my organizer—the disc which I must now be careful never to reformat or over-write. From now on, I had to keep proper track of myself, lest I lose my true past and my authentic being to the ravages of the disease.

What will the historians of the far future make of all these documents? I wondered. *Will they be grateful for the sudden glut of resources, or will they think it insane that we should devote so much painstaking attention to the recording and analysis of events which never happened?*

It was good to have the opportunity to indulge in such idle speculations. This was the first quiet moment I'd had all day: the first chance I'd had to assess my new situation calmly and without distraction. For a little while I was able to congratulate myself on how well I was doing, and how much in control I was, but I couldn't maintain a wholly positive frame of mind. I'd been shaken up by Jill's reaction, which had been worse than I'd expected. I was slowly overtaken by a sense of the enormity of it all.

Where, I wondered, would it end—not just for me but for the whole human world?

I knew that there was a real possibility that I and everyone else alive might lose everything, in spite of all our methodical recording and all our careful vigilance. If the biologists could identify the agent and devise an effective treatment, the plague could still be stopped in its tracks, but if they couldn't it might well keep on expanding its range and its scope. It was all too horribly plausible that the girls and the babies were just a passing phase, like the aliens and the child abusers before them, and that the next wave of fantasies might be altogether less comfortable.

At the moment, I thought, *I'm still the same person I've always been. Knowing Marilyn has hardly changed me at all—but even Marilyn could make a different man of me, if she plays an increasingly important part in my remembrance of things past. What are we, after all, but the sum of our memories? I could be embarked on a process of metamorphosis as profound, its own way, as the one that makes a caterpillar into a butterfly.*

Even that, I realized as soon as I'd formulated the words, was a prettification: an attempt to make what was happening seem harmless, natural and progressive. There were a few enthusiasts on the lunatic fringe who were very fond of the butterfly analogy, proclaiming—as Aileen had briefly suggested in the pub—that the plague was no plague at all, but simply the next step in the evolution of *Homo superior* and the dawning of a new era of self-reconstruction. According to these particular lunatics, courage and cunning would give the bravest of us the ability to take control of the whole process, and thus remake ourselves and the whole world. They rejected the whole philosophy underlying the kind of record-keeping in which I was patiently engaged. CAST OFF THE CHAINS OF YESTERDAY was their slogan; ERASE THE FAULTS OF HISTORY AND WRITE THE WORLD ANEW! Admirable, in its way—except that neither courage nor cunning had yet contrived to make the slightest dent in the capacity which the plague had to defy and deny the consciousness of its victims.

I remembered a day I'd spent in London with Marilyn—a day that never was, when we'd gone to see The Comedy of Errors at the Barbican and then to eat in an Italian restaurant in a paved alleyway off Charing Cross Road. I knew it wasn't in the record I'd made at the weekend, but I felt sure that it was just something that had slipped my mind, something that had been there all along, quietly unexamined, waiting to resurface in response to the right cue. It wasn't a sharp memory, but there was something so extremely lucid about it that it would have been ridiculous to doubt it if I hadn't been so sharply aware of the hazards of FMS.

There's no way I can be absolutely certain, of course, I told myself, teasingly, *that today's memories aren't false from beginning to end. In the final analysis, there's no way I can ever be certain of anything any more. Perhaps my memories of Marilyn are the only real memories I have left, and all that presently surrounds me is just the plague's way of breaking down that last stubborn residue of lost reality. Anyhow, given that the demons of delusion are free to ravage the world, hasn't the empire of reality already fallen? What profit is there in trying to sift the actual from the illusory? Wouldn't it be saner and wiser to make commitments on aesthetic grounds, preferring those memories—true or false—which are the most edifying? What possible reason is there for trying to cast Marilyn out of my past when her presence there is such a rich source of bittersweet satisfaction? Why should I try to contain and confine her, when she only ever wanted to make me happy? It was me who blew it, after all. If only I'd handled things better, we might still be together today....*

Jill put her head around the door, tentatively.

"Are you done yet? Can I come in?" she asked.

I finished the edit and closed the lid of my handbook. "It's okay," I said. "I'm up to date."

She came to stand behind me, and put her hands on my shoulders, squeezing gently. "I'm sorry about downstairs," she said. "I don't know why I reacted like that. I suppose I'd been sort of expecting it, subconsciously, and all this *stuff* had built up, just waiting to explode when you hit the trigger. None of it's your fault—I know that. It's just a disease. It's not as if you can choose whether to get infected or not. I'm truly sorry."

"It's okay," I said. "I understand. It's difficult. But we're sensible, mature adults. If anyone can cope, it's us. It's just a matter of coming to terms with it and seeing it through—*together*."

"That's right," she said. "And when all's said and done, the past is dead and gone. It doesn't matter what happens to the past, as long as the present and the future are secure. Marilyn might be able to steal your memories—even your memories of me—but she can't steal you. I'll always have the flesh and blood, won't I? No matter how many yesterdays she swallows up, I'll still have all the tomorrows."

I knew she must have been rehearsing that speech while she sat on her own downstairs, staring unheedingly at the TV screen.

"That's right," I told her. "That's absolutely right. It's you I really love. It always will be." Was there ever a time when people didn't make such reckless promises? Was there ever a time when people didn't mean them?

"I'll help you," she said, fervently kneading my shoulder muscles with her slender, insistent fingers. "I'll make sure you can't forget what we have. I'll keep on and on reminding you of the way it really was, and the way it really is. I'll never let you go."

"I know," I said. "I'm glad I'm not alone. In a fight like this, the weight of numbers is vital. The power of consensus is what counts in the end. Consensus, and *love*." I knew, though, even as I stressed the word with such scrupulous care, that "true love" doesn't mean "real love" at all; it means *faithful* love, true in the sense of being true to one's promises.

Marilyn had made promises to me just as I had to her: promises we'd never broken, in spite of everything—including their unreality. Even phantom promises mean something, unless and until they're broken. If they can't be forgotten, they shouldn't be.

"Are you coming to bed now?" Jill asked.

"Yes," I said. I was very tired; it had been a bad day, memorable for all the wrong reasons.

"Good," she said. "I'll fix my face and see you there."

"Okay," I answered, patting her hand as she withdrew it from my shoulder.

I continued sitting where I was for a few minutes longer after she'd left.

Perhaps we should have had a child, I thought. *Children are always there, always clamorous, never giving you a moment's peace for self-absorbed reflection. In the end, of course, they leave you— one way or another—but while they're around you really don't have the time to be ill.*

Then I got up and went to the bedroom, wondering what my dreams would make of me, and who I might be when they finally released me to the cold bright light of morning.

INSIDE OUT

"I'M SLIGHTLY DISTURBED by these dreams you've been having," the doctor said, in the solicitous manner he adopted for all his consultations.

"You shouldn't be," Margaret told him. "They frightened me, at first, but they don't any longer."

Doctor Huxley frowned at that. Perhaps he thought that it was impolite of her to stop being frightened of the dreams even though he hadn't yet contrived to explain them. He seemed to have put away his textbook Freud for the time being. Perhaps it would have been kinder had she managed to summon up some forgotten memory of unexpectedly coming across her parents engaged in the sweaty commerce of love, so that he could seize upon it as the commonplace root of her trouble. She had read enough of the great psychotherapist's works to make the fiction convincing, but she didn't want to descend to dishonesty.

"I'm not at all sure that the drug is having the desired effect," the doctor told her. "I'm not sure the people at the Ministry know what they're doing. I think the experiment ought to be stopped, before it does someone harm."

"It's not doing me harm," Margaret assured him. "I thought it might be, at first, but I don't think so now. I think the dreams are helping me, just as you hoped they would. You shouldn't give up the experiment yet."

"*How* do you think the dreams are helping you?" he wanted to know.

Unfortunately, she couldn't tell him. A patient couldn't tell her doctor that what he took for dreams were actually real; she had, after all, been judged at least half-mad, else she wouldn't be here. There were some things that simply couldn't be said, lest they be taken as final proof that her madness was absolute. And yet, she thought, she had the right of it. The dreams were not such stuff as dreams were ordinarily made of, and if she had to rebuild her idea of the world in order to accommodate them, that was what she must do, albeit in secret. Why should she not seek a new reality, after all, given that the one she had inherited had failed her so badly, and wounded her so deeply?

"They're helping me to get *out of myself*," was all she dared say aloud. "They're helping me to see that the frightened creature I'd become, all knotted up and self-enclosed, isn't really me...not the *whole* me, at any rate. It really was a trauma response—something that the war did to me. The dreams are telling me—showing me—that there are other ways to be."

"I wish I could agree with you," the doctor said, although Margaret couldn't for the life of her see why he couldn't. "Unfortunately, it seems to me that the dreams are *symptoms* of trauma response, transfiguring your problems without diminishing them at all. I'm worried that they might actually be making the grip of the trauma more secure. If only we could decode them we might be able to get at the root of the problem, but while we can't...."

"They were distressing at first," Margaret was quick to put in, "and I suppose they're still disturbing—but I don't feel that the disturbance is destructive. Sometimes, surely, it's good to be disturbed, if things have become too tightly-bound, too *fixed*."

"Sometimes," he conceded—although she knew that it was only a doctor's concession, by way of humoring the patient. "In your case, though, I'm not so sure. Distress can be a warning, you know, and it's possible that the easing of your distress is actually a sign that your condition is getting worse."

"I don't think so, doctor," she told him, as patiently as she could. "I think you've got things inside out. I'm feeling better because I'm getting better, beginning to see the light at the end of the tunnel." She turned her head briefly as she heard a sound that might be the drone of a distant aircraft engine, but it was only a house-fly, which had somehow eased its way into the room and was now intent on finding a way out into the afternoon sunlight.

"I'm glad that you feel that way," Doctor Huxley replied, bringing the full weight of his professional insincerity to bear. "It's good that you're feeling better, but however inside out it seems, there's a world of difference between feeling better for a little while and getting better for good. If we've learned anything during the last seventeen years, it's that winning a battle isn't he same as winning a war."

If we've learned anything during the last seventeen years, Margaret thought, *it's that no possible end, no possible victory, no possible settlement, can ever justify the fighting of a war like this one.* She didn't say so out loud, not because it mightn't sound sufficiently sane but because it mightn't sound sufficiently patriotic. Doctor Huxley was, after all, an employee of the Ministry of War. She resorted, instead, to a direct approach.

"Please don't discontinue the treatment, doctor," she said. "I really do think that I'm making progress."

"I wish I could see it," he answered, mournfully. Now he, too, was following the fly's wayward trajectory with his speculative eye.

Perhaps you could, Margaret thought, *if only you weren't so dutifully blind.*

* * * * * * *

SHE IS WALKING through a wood in late spring. The trees are discarding their roseate blossom; their vivid crowns are full of birdsong. The grass is moist with the legacy of recent rain. Her feet leave prints in the soft soil whenever she crosses bare ground.

The prints are those of cloven hooves, although she walks erect as befits a sentient being. Even centaurs hold their true selves erect, although they go on four legs instead on two.

She pauses in the bushes on the edge of a sunlit glade, peeping through a narrow gap so that she may see without being seen.

What she sees is betrayal.

On a bed of moss in the shadow of a gnarled oak a male faun is lying beside a shy nymph. The nymph averts her face from the tentative caress of his hairy hand, although the glint in her green eyes reveals to the watcher that the touch is not unwelcome. One of the faun's shaggy legs reaches out so that the hoof may tease and tickle the back of the nymph's calf; she quivers slightly, but not in anguish, and makes no attempt to rise to her feet.

Why, the watcher wonders, is it always thus? Why do fauns prefer such creatures to their own kind? It makes no sense; it is a jarring note in the great litany of Harmony.

As her jealous heart beats faster, the watcher feels a sudden unease. She looks to the side, where she has seen some movement from the corner of her eye. There, emerging from a thicket not unlike the one in which she herself is hiding, is a creature born of nightmares. It walks erect like any sentient being but its face is utterly brutal, worse than the face of the hoariest of the Sileni. Its hide is dark and its joints glint metallically. Its heavy clothing is coarse. Upon its back it carries a curious cylinder from which extends a flexible hose connected to the tub its bears in its horrid hands.

For a single fleeting second, the watcher thinks: *It is justice, after all. Do they not deserve it?*

She has no time to repent the flash of wrath before the monster changes course, abruptly turning its attention to her. She sees the mouth of the tube pointed directly at her, and she sees the great gout of flame which vomits out of it, hurtling to engulf her.

She never feels the heat, let alone the pain, of her own conflagration—but she knows how terrible it must be to melt and to burn, to be utterly consumed by fire and fury.

She knows...and she carries that knowledge with her through dimensions unknown to those she has saved, unsuspected by those who will now escape to continue their betrayal, their defiance of all that is or ought to be sacred.

* * * * * * *

"WHERE, EXACTLY, DID this come from, Dr. Reed?" Fowler wanted to know.

"Parallel 4972B3," Joanna told him. "My *alter ego* there is fully controlled and active. We're using her to direct experiments in psychic boosting using a variety of drugs. There's a sanatorium in Winchelsea in Southern England, set up to treat what they call trauma response. They discarded the term shellshock when they decided that it really was a medical problem and not disguised cowardice. The doctor in charge—a man named Huxley—thinks he's exploring the therapeutic potential of various psychotropic drugs under the direction of the War Ministry. This is the only patient of his who's so far shown any indication of an ability to make contact with her alternative selves."

Joanna could tell that Fowler wasn't in the least impressed. He'd been part of the project since its inception, long before Joanna's time. For all she knew, he might be the oldest of the Old Guard. His idea of a field agent was one who swashed and buckled her way through a hundred action-filled parallel lives, changing local history left right and centre in the hallowed name of progress, not one who conducted experiments in psychometry using the parallels as samples and controls.

"So this is an account of a dream reported by one of Huxley's patients?" he said, in his annoyingly punctilious fashion, looking down his nose at the text.

"A drug-assisted dream, yes. Induced by a laboratory derivative of psilocin—that's a fungal alkaloid, similar to psilocybin but lacking a phosphate group."

Fowler was not the kind of man to worry about such trivial details as the presence or absence of a phosphate group. "And why do you think it's of any interest to us?"

Joanna fought to remain perfectly calm, telling herself that it really wasn't Fowler's fault. He simply had an imaginative allergy to data that didn't fit the patterns which the mapmakers were spinning out of the scanning data. It was a medical problem, like any other quirk of brain chemistry.

"What she's describing," Joanna said, carefully keeping her voice neutral, "is a soldier with a flame-thrower. A soldier from one of the Imperialist parallels on Axis C."

"That's absurd!" Fowler retorted. "This is the stuff of fantasy! The dreamer can't possibly be contacting an alternative self. She's imagining herself as some kind of female satyr! We've no evidence of the existence of such beings in any of the parallels we've scanned, even as far out as the D axis."

"That depends what counts as evidence," Joanna countered, with painstaking mildness. "We know that most, if not all, of the parallels we've scanned have legends relating to such creatures. The consistency and everpresence of such legends surely suggests that they might actually exist somewhere in the continuum, and that intelligence of their existence is leaking through the mindweb."

Fowler had no sympathy with the school of thought which held that all fantasy was simply altereality glimpsed through the dark glass of multiple self-awareness. He was a pragmatist, who worried far more about the Imperialist threat to the A and B axes than the possibility that their adventures might extend into *terrae incognitae*.

"That's nonsense," he informed her, loftily "If the consistency and everpresence of such legends has any bearing at all on the possible existence of mythical creatures it assures us that they belong entirely to the distant past. One of the few things we know for sure about the multiverse is the consistency of the moment. Insofar as other parallels are accessible to us, they're only accessible to us at precisely complementary points in time. The other selves with which psychics can make contact always exist at an exactly similar point in time."

"Once you grant the possibility that they did exist," Joanna countered, stubbornly, "then it's surely possible that there are a few parallels—albeit distant from the ones we can most easily explore—where such creatures still exist in the everpresent today."

"We've found no evidence of such parallels," Fowler stated, flatly.

"This *is* evidence," Joanna told him, losing the battle to control her impatience. "You're just refusing to acknowledge it as such. If you won't allow any such evidence to be considered, it's hardly surprising that it can't subsequently be found, is it? Given that your primary interest is in the parallels most like our own it's entirely understandable that you should focus your attention and your pattern-analyses on axes A and B, but that doesn't mean that there aren't far stranger parallels, which are far more difficult for our psychics to contact—so much more difficult that they might require the assistance of psychotropic drugs. Surely there's ample room in a truly infinite multiverse for all kinds of alternative humankinds...." She was careful enough not to add "undreamt of in your philosophy"—not out loud, anyway.

"You can't have it both ways," Fowler informed her, with the predatory air of one who has found a crucial logical flaw in his opponent's argument. "If you're using the alleged presence of an Imperialist soldier to validate this hallucination, you're presuming that this parallel lies close enough to their home bases to permit the large-scale conscription of male *alter egos*. It simply doesn't fit, Dr. Reed. It doesn't fit at all."

"I know it doesn't fit with present theory," Joanna retorted, still trying her utmost to keep her voice level. "The point is, does it not fit because it's just a dream whose connections to our other explorations arise out of mere coincidence, or does it not fit because our tentative theories are too narrow to encompass the true hyperdimensional geometry and the whole range of phenomena which the multiverse accommodates? If there's the slightest possibility that the latter is the case, we ought to investigate further and more scrupulously, don't you think?"

Joanna could see in the old man's face that his answer was a flat *no*, but even Fowler felt that he ought to prevaricate a little, for safety's sake. No one worked half a lifetime in a madhouse like this without learning to cover his arse. "Tell me about the dreamer's parallel," he said, warily. "What's the state of play there?"

"Huxley's sanatorium is well-supplied with patients because the Great War's still going on."

"Still! That's very unusual."

"But hardly unprecedented." Joanna knew that Fowler had been party to the grand fiasco of 4821B1, where a botched attempt by a handful of agents to bring an unnaturally-extended Great War to its "natural" end had instead resulted in the outbreak of the most devastating Plague War ever recorded. The memory of it must still rankle, but his features were frozen, permitting no acknowledgement of the point she had scored.

"The patient's a twenty-six-year-old woman who was working as a nursing auxiliary in Flanders for some years before being sent home," Joanna went on. "If she hadn't been invalided out, of course, she'd have been killed or captured when Ludendorff finally drove the allies out of continental Europe. Since then he's been sending wave after wave of zeppelin bombers against London, trying to finish the job. Strays must go back and forth over Winchelsea all the time, offering the patients uncomfortable reminders of the conflict, but it's a relatively quiet spot."

"But this woman was close to the front for some considerable time," Fowler said. "She must have seen men with flame-throwers and she must have seen their victims. She must also have seen men with protective clothing and gas masks. I presume they're still using phosgene and chlorine as weapons?"

"Worse than that," Joanna conceded. "They introduced Lewisite before France fell; now the zeppelins have brought gas warfare to the streets of London, as well as a new generation of incendiary weapons. I think they call them inflammatols. Not the sort of stuff I'd want to lug around under a hydrogen-filled gasbag the size of a football pitch, but that's modern warfare axis-B style."

Fowler obviously didn't approve of the slight note of flippancy in this last remark. "She's not describing an Imperialist conscript," he said, his voice redolent with unwarranted certainty. "She's merely describing a German soldier—one of those who might well be about to invade and spoil England's green and pleasant land. I don't know why she sees herself as a female satyr, but I'm as sure as I can be that it's not because she has another self in some fugitive corner of the multiverse who *is* a female satyr. Come back to me if and when you've got something to show me, Dr. Reed. In my view, your team ought to abandon the experiments with psilocin and psilocybin. So far as I can see, there's no evidence at all to suggest that they can boost the latent powers of uncultivated psychics."

The last gratuitous insult nearly cracked Joanna's self-control again, but she managed to restrict the damage to a filthy look. She kept her lips resolutely sealed as she collected her files as she stalked out of the room. Not until she was well clear of the great man's office did she begin to let the pent-up emotion go, and even then the obscenities she poured down upon his stubborn head were silent ones.

* * * * * * *

SHE IS WALKING along a dusty road, longing for the sight on an inn-sign swaying in the warm breeze. The tall hedges to either side of the road conceal fields where the wheat grows tall. Those fields are on the point of turning from a uniform vivid green to the mottled maturity which invites the harvest.

The basket in her arms seems to grow heavier with every step.

As she rounds a shallow bend in the road she stumbles in the rut left by a cartwheel. She staggers into the hedge, which welcomes her into its ungentle embrace. From this position she can see around the bend, and what she sees is betrayal.

A young man is there, sitting languidly on a stile with his head tilted back, so that a lamia might stroke his neck with her clawed fingers. He is looking up into her face; the expression in his eyes suggests that she has required no stupefying magic to subdue him.

The watcher remains quite still, accepting the roughness of the twigs which dig into her flesh. She cannot tear her eyes away. Her gaze takes in the seductive expression in the face of the silver-haired temptress with the lustrous skin and the tiny fangs, and its counter-part in the lustful eyes of the young man.

Why, the watcher wonders, is it always thus? Why do men pre-fer such creatures to their own kind? It makes no sense; it is a jarring note in the great litany of Harmony.

Then she sees something beyond the oblivious pair—something which is approaching at terrible speed.

It is some kind of cart which moves thunderously upon huge patterned wheels, without any horse to haul it. It is manned by mon-sters with vile, inhuman masks instead of faces, and there is some-thing about their bodies which seems to be more or less than flesh. One of them is pointing a metal wand at the young man and the snake-girl,

For a single fleeting second, the watcher thinks: *It is justice, af-ter all. Do they not deserve it?*

Even as the couple turn to look at the approaching vehicle, however, the monster redirects the device to aim it at the watcher's fluttering heart—and the magical cart sweeps past the stile, heading straight for her.

She hears the roar of the wand. She never sees the missiles hurled from its tip, but she knows how terrible it must be to be torn apart, to be ripped and shattered and blasted into shreds.

She knows...and she carries that knowledge with her through dimensions unknown to those she has saved, unsuspected by those who will now escape to continue their betrayal, their defiance of all that is or ought to be sacred.

* * * * * *

ANDREW HUXLEY STOOD on the lawn outside the west wing of the sanatorium, watching the huge silver cigar sliding towards the southern horizon. It was belatedly pursued by a brace of Avro fighters. The Zeppelin's escort of Fokkers and Spads has been reduced by half—the aerial battle which raged every day above the Weald must have been unusually fierce—but Andrew knew that the Avros had little chance of weaving a way through them to come within range of their prime target. If only the machine guns mounted on their wings had greater power! If only the anti-aircraft guns that ringed the capital could be fired with greater accuracy!

He turned around as Joanna Reed came up behind him, making sure that he could meet her eyes before she spoke. There was something very disconcerting about the woman; she gave the impression of concealing hidden depths, although she was supposedly a very minor cog in the mighty machine of the War Ministry. He suspected that she was some kind of agent for Military Intelligence.

"All monoplanes," he said, lightly enough. "We never see biplanes any more, do we? When my father fought with the Army Air Force most Fokkers had three wings, but everything is becoming simpler now, more streamlined. War's good for progress, they say. Ten years more and we'll have such a cornucopia of technical skills that we'll be able to murder our enemies as easily as our combine harvesters mow down fields of wheat."

"No doubt we will," the woman said, with awesome matter-of-factness, "but that's not what I'm here to talk about."

Had the bureaucrats in Whitehall really become so completely inured to the destruction which was being rained down upon them, Andrew wondered. Had they now accepted the war as a mere condition of existence? Or was theirs simply a different kind of trauma response?

"Why are you here?" he asked.

"Your request to discontinue Margaret Lane's treatment landed on my desk. I'm here to deny it. Such a move would be severely deleterious to the experiment."

"It's not the experiment that concerns me, Miss Reed," Andrew told her, making every effort to keep his voice calm and reasonable. "You have to remember that I'm a doctor, and that my first duty is to my patients. I agreed to take part in your testing program because

46

you persuaded me that the drugs you supply might have a therapeutic effect. In some cases, I admit, they do seem to have helped a little—but not in Margaret's. These drug-induced dreams are disturbing her; far from becoming calmer, she's becoming more agitated and more uncooperative. I can't seem to get through to her any more—she's become furtive and deceptive, and I'm worried that she might be descending into psychosis. I can't in all conscience administer any further doses to her."

"If we're to make a proper judgment regarding the utility of psychotropic medicine," the woman told him, without a flicker of embarrassment, "the experiment must be conducted along proper scientific lines. It must run its entire course."

"Not if it endangers the wellbeing of my patients," Andrew insisted. "For God's sake, woman, don't you think they've gone through enough already? These men and women have been to Hell, and they haven't yet come all the way back. I'm not interested in the integrity and rigor of your research program; my only concern is to alleviate the suffering of the men and women in my care."

She obviously wasn't impressed by his increasing vehemence. "If we're ever to understand the phenomena of trauma response, Dr. Huxley, we must examine it very carefully and very scrupulously. Until we can understand it, we can't hope to cure it. In any case, there doesn't seem to us to be any cause for alarm; there's no firm evidence that Miss Lane's condition is deteriorating."

She always speaks of "we" and "us", Andrew thought. *It's always impersonal. But who, exactly, is "us"? Whose spokesman is she? To whom is she responsible?*

"How can you say that there's no firm evidence?" he complained. "You've read the accounts of those dreams she's having—indeed, you seem to have read them with great avidity. How can you ignore the signs of disturbance they display?"

"They're only dreams," the woman said, although there was a curious glint in her eye which somehow suggested that she didn't mean what she said.

"Dreams are meaningful," Andrew countered. "They offer us an invaluable window into the depths of the unconscious, if only we can take the trouble to unravel their symbolism. When a person continually dreams of meeting a horrible death it tells me that my patient is far from well, Miss Reed, and getting worse. I'd be a fool—*we*'d be fools—to ignore these ominous signs."

"What else do Miss Lane's dreams tell you, Dr. Huxley?" she asked, in a manner which suggested that she wasn't going to believe his answer.

"They tell me that the fear of death that has already blighted Margaret's capacity for rational thought and action is on the point of obliterating her sanity altogether," he told her, with what he hoped was disarmingly brutal frankness. "The war for continental Europe may seem to have been a mere matter of moving colored pins around on a map to you, Miss Reed, but to her it was something *real*. It was something going on all around her, year after year, eating away at her inner being until there was nothing left but some little beleaguered island of self—and the injections of psilocin I've been giving her at your request have been the equivalent of Ludendorff's accursed zeppelins, clawing away at that little island's defenses. If I don't stop—if *we* don't stop—she'll be lost forever."

"Forever's a long time, Dr. Huxley," Joanna Reed informed him, with a gravity whose blatant insincerity was insulting. "As a matter of interest, though, I wonder what you make of the settings of Miss Lane's dreams, and the manner in which she populates those settings."

"The settings are always pastoral," Andrew replied, wondering whether the best chance of getting what he wanted might be to play along with her, at least for a while. "They always contain elements borrowed from mythology—sometimes quite abstruse elements, although Margaret never had any kind of Classical education. They always include a male figure whose dalliance with a female of some subtly different species distresses her. They obviously refer to some unfortunate incident in her past, but she's resisted all my attempts to identify it. It must have been something that happened in Flanders— at a guess, I'd say that she became romantically involved with some young soldier, then suffered a violent reaction when she saw him with someone else—a whore, maybe. I don't want to put ideas into her head by asking leading questions, but I've tried find out whether something of that kind happened by subtler means and I've got nowhere. What I do know, for certain, is that it's doing her no good to relive that moment over and over again, constantly linking it up to images of her own violent death."

"We need more data," the woman insisted, placidly. "We have to keep on collecting it. There may be much more at stake here than you realize."

"No," Andrew said, trying as hard as he could to sound equally definite and equally stubborn, "you're wrong about that. I know that it's not just a matter of one mentally ill girl. I know that there's been a war on for seventeen years, and that its recent phases have produced cases of traumatic response by the trainload. I know what's at stake. It's people like you—people who have become so inured to the idea of mass slaughter that the war's become a mere matter of statistics and strategies—who don't realize that what's really at stake and always has been at stake and always will be at stake is people's lives and people's minds. I can't stop you thinking of all those young boys you send out with guns and tanks and bombs and aeroplanes as mere cannon-fodder to be sacrificed wholesale in your *great cause*, but I can make a stand for my patients and I will. I won't feed that poor girl any more of your mind-bending rubbish, and I won't let you do it either."

"I'm sorry you feel that way," said Joanna Reed, "but you really don't have any choice. We need the data, and we intend to have it. It really is important."

Overhead, a lone Avro was returning from it expedition over the blue-grey waters of the channel. The drone of its engine sounded unreasonably waspish as it overflew the sanatorium.

"Sometimes," Andrew said, softly, "I think my patients are the only sane people left in the world. They're the only ones who see things as they really are, in all their unspeakable and unbearable horror. We're the mad ones, because we're the ones who screen that horror out and concentrate our minds on keeping the war going, on killing more and more people more and more quickly. Perhaps you and I are the sick people, Miss Reed. Perhaps Margaret Lane is the one who can see clearly, in her traumatized imagination."

He had thought that Joanna Reed didn't have the capacity to surprise him, but she surprised him then. She was already turning to walk away, and her reply seemed not to be addressed to him at all, but she did reply.

What she said was: "That's exactly why we have to carry on."

* * * * * * *

RECENTLY RETURNED TO human form, she kneels by the stream and scoops up water with which to wash her face. There is always a period of disorientation while her thinking mind regains its forsaken empire; sometimes, just for a few minutes, she retains some memory of what it is like to go on all fours and to live without sentience. It is those precious minutes which inform her of the secret and sacred truth that it is better by far to live as a wolf than as a human being. Wolves are conscious, but not of themselves; they possess—and are possessed by—emotions, but they have no thoughts to spoil the ecstasy of their existence.

She looks up when she hears laughter coming from behind a dense clump of bulrushes that grows where the stream widens into a pool. She moves towards the rushes, crawling on all fours as though she were still a wolf. She peeps discreetly through the curtain of vegetation.

What she sees is betrayal. A male wolf is there, sporting with a female—but the female is a wolf through and through, and the male is not. The male is of the *vargr*-folk. He does not know what he is doing, of course—but that is no excuse.

Why, the watcher wonders, is it always thus? Why do were-wolves prefer such creatures to their own kind? It makes no sense; it is a jarring note in the great litany of Harmony.

She wants to rise to her feet, but she is afraid that if she does so, the wolves will see her as prey, and might attack.

A noise behind her causes her to look around.

The thing that is coming towards her is a travesty of a man, but there is hardly any flesh about it and its face is utterly evil—not hungry, like the face of a wolf, but something much worse.

For a single fleeting second, the watcher thinks: *It is justice, after all. Do they not deserve it?* But she sees that the creature's un-human eyes are fixed on her.

From its hand of polished steel the monster launches a spinning cylinder, which turns over and over in the air, catching the sunlight, before it falls into the water beside her and begins hissing madly. The gas released from within turns the placid stream to turbulent foam.

She never feels the silent enemy gripping her throat and her lungs, but she knows how frightful it must be to have the quiet chemistry of one's being violently disrupted, to have poisons surging through one's blood, devouring one's very soul.

She knows...and she carries that knowledge with her through dimensions unknown to those she has saved, unsuspected by those who will now escape to continue their betrayal, their defiance of all that is or ought to be sacred.

* * * * * * *

"GET DRESSED, MARGARET. We have to leave now."

Dr. Huxley's voice was unnaturally calm; Margaret could tell that he was trying to give the impression of being in complete control, but she knew that he was fooling himself.

"You don't understand, doctor," she told him, making every effort to match his appearance of calm. "I know what's happening now."

He thrust a bundle of clothes towards her: it included a grey skirt and a starched white blouse; blue socks and brown shoes. She already had her underwear on, beneath her nightdress; it was a habit she'd acquired in Flanders and never let go. It was always wise to be ready, in case something untoward happened that required a rapid response.

Dr. Huxley obviously thought that something untoward had happened, but it hadn't. This was a safe place—as safe as any could be, given the nature of the world, and the nature of the worlds beyond the world.

"I've figured it out," she told him, as she began to put the clothes on, taking her time so that she'd have time to spell things out. "At first I thought the others were *in* me, but they're not. At first I thought I'd been splintered into a hundred or a thousand selves by some kind of bomb exploding in my mind, but I had it all inside out. I really do have a thousand or a million other selves, but the ones close at hand are all screaming, all in agony. Even the ones that are furthest away are under threat. I'm being hunted, you see, doctor... hunted across a million or a billion worlds. It was supposed to be over long ago, doctor—three thousand years ago, or maybe more. All the chimeras' children were hunted down, everywhere they existed...but some of them weren't so easy to detect, and there are more worlds than anyone ever imagined...worlds beyond the worlds beyond the world. *They* think they're everywhere, but they can't really be everywhere, because everywhere's *too large*. No matter what they see, there's always an infinity that lies beyond, glimpsed but essentially unseen. No matter how long the Imperial adventure goes on, it will always be continuing; no part of the work can ever be complete, because there's always somewhere where it's only just beginning."

"Come on, Margaret," said Dr. Huxley, softly, as she finally had to finish tying her shoelaces. "I'm going to need your help now. We have to get away from here tonight. I've found a place for you to hide—a place where they'll look after you, and give you a proper chance to recover. There'll be no more drugs, and the dreams will gradually die away. It'll help a lot if you try to forget them, and try to stop searching them for some kind of cosmic truth which simply isn't there."

While he was speaking Dr. Huxley led her out of the room and down the corridor. She tried to hold back but he wouldn't let her. While they were going down the stairs and through the hall she continued trying to explain, although she knew in her heart of hearts that he wasn't capable of listening to what she said, and couldn't even begin to take any of it seriously.

"It's not the drugs, doctor," she told him. "They just helped to trip the switch. I don't need them any more; they've done their work. Once the contact is made, it becomes much easier to maintain. If only my nearer selves were living peaceful lives I could borrow some of their stability, their peace of mind—but they're not, and they're mostly in such terrible distress that I have to start...well, not at the *other end* because there *is* no end, but at a level of contact that's much slighter...so slight that it wouldn't be achievable if it weren't for the horrid necessity of avoiding everything closer at hand. I wish you'd listen to me, doctor, because it really is important. If I could only make you understand...."

They were outside now. The night was cloudy and the windows of the sanatorium were blacked out; only the hall light, shining through the open door, lit the way to the doctor's battered Morris.

"Get into the car, Margaret," Dr. Huxley said, still speaking with the carefully-contrived voice of masculine authority. "Just get into the car, and try to stay calm."

Try to stay calm! If only he knew what the price of calmness was! If only he could see that the awesomely simple world he inhabited was simple only because he was blind to its myriad alternatives, and that the sanity he valued so highly was nothing but determined ignorance of the actual nature of the universe...of the multiverse. If only he could catch a glimpse, if only for a instant, of the vast spectrum of Dr. Huxleys that extended across the vast spectrum of the worlds which contained him: the thriving and the dying; the wise and the foolish; the joyous and the despairing; the pain-racked and the....

The car engine wouldn't start. Dr. Huxley reached under the seat for the crank-handle that had to be inserted in the hole beneath the radiator grille, so that he could turn it over by hand, forcing life into it by the power of muscle and will. That was what he tried to do with his patients. He thought of them as recalcitrant engines, which needed to be started by the power of muscle and will.

"You don't understand, Dr. Huxley," she told him. "I can see now. I was blind, but you helped me to see. I know now what the world is really like, and what I really am. None of us is alone, Dr. Huxley—we only think we are because we can't make contact with our other selves. Maybe that's a good thing, in a way, because there's so much pain out there and so much confusion. Everybody is dying *somewhere*, everybody is screaming in pain somewhere, everybody is something they don't want to be, everybody is something they don't even believe in, everybody is everywhere and everything and it simply isn't bearable unless you can somehow get past the ones who are hurting...even then, it isn't easy, especially when they're the nearest ones, but it can be done...."

The engine wouldn't start. Dr. Huxley kept turning the handle, but it only went *clunk*, like something dead and leaden.

"I'm sorry, Dr. Huxley," said a new voice, "but I really can't allow you to do this."

Dr. Huxley dropped the crank-handle and whipped around. His composure had vanished on the instant and he was all panic now. Margaret recognized the woman who'd spoken; she was called Joanna, and she was a regular visitor at the sanatorium. Recently, she'd taken quite an interest in Margaret and her dreams. It was almost as if she understood what was happening to her.

Unfortunately, *almost* wasn't good enough.

Margaret didn't recognize the two men Joanna had with her. They reminded her of policemen or army officers because of the way they carried themselves, but they weren't in uniform. That was surprising—almost all men of their age were in uniform nowadays. There was a war on.

In fact, there were more wars on than they could possibly imagine, and bigger ones too.

Margaret heard the purr of an engine then, but it wasn't the engine of Dr. Huxley's car; it was the engine of an aeroplane high in the sky. She couldn't see it, because the night was too dark, but she strained her ears, trying to figure out which way it was going.

It was coming nearer, from the northwest, and it wasn't alone. She could hear other engines: several high-pitched ones, and one that sounded a deeper, calmer note.

"She's my patient," Dr. Huxley said to Joanna. "My only duty is to her."

"You know that's not true, Dr. Huxley," Joanna replied. "Your first duty is to your country, which is at war. Violation of that duty is called treason."

Margaret took leave to wonder what all the other Joannas were like, even though she knew that it was a meaningless question. There were so many Joannas that they were like anything and everything. Somewhere, there must be Joannas who knew that they were not the only Joannas. Somewhere, there might be a Joanna who knew exactly what this Joanna was doing, and maybe even why. That Joanna would doubtless consider herself to be the wisest of all the Joannas, and her world the ultimate world of all: the baseline of the entire multiverse...but she'd be wrong, because she couldn't possibly be right. The multiverse was simply too big, too nearly infinite, to be based on any single way of thinking, any simple way of being. In the multiverse, everything that could be true *had to be* true; only fools and madmen could ever hope to impose some tyranny of similarity upon its infinite variety.

"You have all the answers, don't you?" Dr. Huxley said. "The war justifies everything you want to do, however cruel or crazy. The menace of Ludendorff licenses any mad whim that happens to cross your bureaucratic little mind. You don't realize that you've already lost. Even if you win in the end, you've lost—because you've surrendered to the principle of the end justifying the means."

"Get out of the car, Miss Lane," Joanna said.

Margaret didn't see why Joanna had to be so formal; she'd always called her Margaret before.

The cacophony that possessed the sky had become much louder now; the noise of the aeroplane engines was overlain by the mad chattering of machine-guns. As Margaret stepped out of the car she looked up into the dark sky, where not a single star shone through the clouds. She knew that the invisible stars were there, though: thousands upon thousands of them. She knew, too, that beyond the thousands which could be counted were millions more...and beyond them, billions. There was no end to the universe of stars save for that imposed upon it by the limits of human vision.

I don't understand why my nearer selves are all screaming, Margaret thought, as she stared up at the smothering curtain of the dark, looking for the tiny pinpricks and threads of light which would be the Avros and the Sopwiths and the Spads and the Fokkers firing and firing and firing at one another with the aid of their brand new night-sights. *Surely it can't be like that for everyone who learns to see. Surely some of them must find that their nearest and dearest selves are happy and healthy and full of life.*

The sky caught fire.

For a moment, Margaret thought that it really was *the sky* that was burning: that the entire vault of Heaven, with all its stars, seen and unseen, had begun to burn. Then she realized that the zeppelin which had been trying to slip back across the channel had been caught by its pursuers, and that its gargantuan gasbag had been breached by tracer-fire. The hydrogen in the envelope had ignited, and turned into a beautiful burning cloud.

Hydrogen, she knew, was lighter than air. The cloud would rise as it burned, heading towards infinity.

The envelope of the zeppelin, alas, was much heavier than air. It fell, along with the car and the engines, dragging terrible billows of fire down to the waiting earth.

Why, she wondered, *is it always thus? It makes no sense. There's no justice in it at all. But the multiverse is the multiverse; there's no great litany of Harmony, nor could there ever be, no matter how we might desire it in our foolishness. There's only chance and change, ebb and flow, birth and rebirth, extinction and creation, darkness and the light. There's only everything.*

Margaret didn't panic when she realized where the debris would fall, and what the consequences of its fall would be. Dr. Huxley and Joanna were panicking, trying to run away even though they didn't know which way to go, but Margaret stayed where she was, shrugging off the clawing hand that Dr. Huxley reached out to her, half-heartedly, as he turned to run. He couldn't even begin to imagine what was about to happen to him, but that only added to his terror. The woman, on the other hand, had a slightly different glint in her eye, as if she *could* begin—but only just—to grasp the triviality as well as the enormity of it all.

Margaret, by contrast, knew exactly what it would be like to burn and to scream. She even knew what it would be like for that scream to echo across the dimensions, unsuspected by those who might escape to continue their petty betrayals and their stubborn defiance of all that was or ought to be sacred.

She knew, too, that in the furthest reaches of the multiverse, there were selves even stranger than the selves which were the stuff of legend. She knew that there were selves stranger than she could ever imagine, who were never in pain and never in danger, some of whom would never, ever die. They were not her like her at all, and yet they *were* her, and their great and infinite community could not be threatened by her own obliteration or the obliteration of a hundred thousand like her. This was not the immortality promised to her by the Church, but it was a kind of immortality worth knowing and worth savoring.

As the burning debris cascaded down upon them all, casually smashing the two running figures to the ground, Margaret thought that it did not matter, after all, whether there was any justice in the world or not. As her flesh melted on her bones, she took more comfort from that thought than she had ever known before, or had ever been likely to know.

AFTER THE STONE AGE

Mina had tried them all: weight-watchers, Conley, grapefruit, Atkins, hypnotherapy and pumping iron. On the day she decided, after three grueling months, that the Stone Age diet was doing her more harm than good—just like all the rest—she felt that she had hit rock bottom in the abyss of despair. She clocked in at sixteen stone five pounds, just six pounds lighter than the day she had embarked on the Stone Age with such steely determination. By the end of March she would doubtless crack the seventeen stone barrier, going in the wrong direction.

Younger people, she supposed, calculated in kilograms but she had never contrived to adjust. Mercifully, she was in public finance rather than the commercial sector, so she rarely had to audit accounts that were connected, even in the remotest degree, with the EU. She never traveled abroad, because she couldn't bear the thought of an aeroplane seat, let alone stripping down to a bikini on a beach in Marbella. She had never lost the habits of embarrassment gained in childhood, and now she had the prospect of middle age spread looming before her.

Mina hadn't an atom of proof that she had been passed over for promotion because of the way she looked. The fact that her newly-imported line manager, Lucy Stanwere, had a figure like Paula Radcliffe as well as being ten years younger might have been coincidence. The fact that Lucy was able to wear four-inch heels, thus allowing her to tower over those condemned by gravity to flat soles, might also irrelevant to her rapid ascent of the status ladder. The fact that Mina was due to see Lucy for her annual appraisal the morning after she fell off the Stone Age wagon and gorged herself on Welsh rarebit and chocolate milk was, however, definitely not a coincidence. Anxiety had always been a key factor in Mina's comfort eating.

Lucy's office was, of course, incredibly neat. It wasn't just that the cleaners made more effort there than in the open-plan, but that

Lucy's own personal neatness radiated out from her size ten suit to bathe her entire environment with a kind of bloodless perfection. Simply being there made Mina feel even more like a rubbish-heap than usual; from the moment she stepped through the door her one ambition was to escape as soon as possible, no matter how much criticism she had to absorb and acknowledge in order to do it. She didn't, of course, dare to entertain the ambition that she might accomplish that escape without some slighting reference being made to her appearance—in fact, the first thing Lucy said, after "Please sit down, Miss Mint," was "Are you unwell?" That, in health-fascist-ese, meant: "How can you even breathe when you're carrying so much excess baggage, you disgusting calorie-addict?"

"I've had a little tummy-trouble recently," Mina admitted, "but it's sure to clear up now."

"Coming off the Stone Age?" Lucy asked, in a tone that sounded almost sympathetic.

Mina had never talked to Lucy in a non-work context, so she couldn't claim to know her well, but she certainly hadn't expected sympathy. She decided that it must be an illusion.

"Yes, actually," Mina admitted.

"I thought so," Lucy said. "The trouble with all these theories about what evolution shaped our digestive systems to do is that humans are so exceedingly adaptable. We grow up on grains and dairy products, and our bodies learn to love them. If there's one thing that separates humans from all the other animals, it's the ability to learn to love. Don't you agree?"

The chance would be a fine thing, Mina thought. What she said aloud was: "Yes, Miss Stanwere."

"It's Lucy. Look, Mina, I don't want to seem presumptuous, and I'll understand if you want to confine our discussion to the nerves and sinews of auditing practice and Gordon Brown's latest wrinkles, but there's a better way to lose weight, if you really want to. It's about time that you were let in on the secret."

Mina had long suspected that there must be a vast conspiracy of the fit and thin whose precious secrets were sternly withheld from people like her, but she had never expected to let into it. She said nothing.

"I know what you're thinking," Lucy Stanwere said, when the pause had passed from pregnant to egg-bound. "How would I know? Well, I do." She took up her handbag. Any normal person would have had to root about for at least thirty seconds to find what she wanted, but Lucy only required a mere moment to pluck the desired item from its innermost depths. She handed Mina a photograph.

Mina stared at the snapshot in frank disbelief. It wasn't so much the sixteen stone version of Lucy Stanwere that startled and appalled her so much as the expression the teenager was wearing: an expression of profound shame and terror of exposure that Mina had only ever seen at weight-watchers—or in a mirror.

When she looked up again, Mina saw her superior with entirely new eyes. She could find but one word: "How?"

Lucy's perfectly-manicured fingers dipped into the mysterious bag for a second time, and produced another slim item. At first, Mina judged from its size that it was a business-card, but it was glossy and black, and bore an image of two magnificently athletic individuals dancing what appeared to be the tango, above the red-lettered inscription:

THE AFTER DARK CLUB

The postcode attached to the address was suggestive of Mayfair.

"Meet me there at ten-thirty," Lucy said. "I'll tell the desk to expect you, and I'll take you in."

"A *night club?*" Mina said, aghast. "I can't go to a night club."

"Ten-thirty," Lucy Stanwere repeated, insistently. "Be on time."

* * * * * * *

MINA HAD NOTHING suitable to wear, but the situation was so surreal that it didn't seem to matter. She was usually curled up in bed with a Mills and Boon not long after ten-thirty, once she'd watched the news on the BBC, so she went to catch the Central Line tube at Ealing Broadway with the kind of disturbed feeling that changes in a familiar routine always bring on.

She had never realized that the urban wilderness between Piccadilly and Oxford Street had so many hidden trails and discreet coverts but her pocket A-to-Z eventually guided her to an unmarked door with a discreet intercom and bell-push. Mina almost turned round and went home right then, but eventually plucked up courage to press the button. When a fuzzy voice said "Yes?" she blurted out "Is-that-the-After-Dark-Club-Lucy-Stanwere-asked-me-to-meet-her-here?" without the slightest pause for breath.

There was an eerie buzzing sound—more like a swarm of angry wasps than placid bees, but no less welcome for that—punctuated by a click. Mina pushed the door open, and entered a gloomy corridor which led to a flight of stairs. At the top of the stairs was a desk, manned by a teenage male in an absurdly old-fashioned suit. "Miss

Mint?" he said, before she could gather her breath. "We've been expecting you. It's a pleasure to meet you."

Mina had not had time to frame a reply when the burgundy-colored door to the left of the desk opened and Lucy Stanwere came out, accompanied by two other men, each as callow as the receptionist, both complexioned like Turks or Italians. They too were wearing black suits cut to standards of formality that had surely gone out with the last King George, or maybe Queen Victoria.

Lucy, by contrast, was dressed in a very *now* manner that was far more relaxed—*louche*, even—than her everyday office-wear. "Mina, darling!" she said, with a brazen bonhomie that contrasted just as sharply with the flinty face of public finance. "I want you to meet Marcian and Szandor. You'll have to forgive Szandor—I'm afraid his English is a trifle rusty—but Marcian will translate for him. Come through, won't you?"

Mina was unable to respond to this invitation immediately, because Marcian and Szandor were busy kissing her hands, so enthusiastically that they hadn't waited to take turns, seizing one apiece. Nor did they let go when they had finished, arranging themselves to either side of her with an affectionate politeness that she had never encountered before. She had, of course, avoided making eye-contact, her embarrassment being so intense that she had all but closed her eyes, but as she stole sidelong glances to her left and right she observed that both of them were looking at her with expressions that betrayed not the slightest hint of disgust, contempt, scorn or disapproval. If she had only dared, she might have felt a surge of joy, but she had lived in the world too long to be free of the suspicion that she was about to suffer some humiliating reversal of fortune.

Marcian and Szandor escorted her through the doorway, although it didn't seem humanly possible that there was room enough for either to pass through it beside her, let alone both. She was swept along another purple-carpeted corridor to another darkly-varnished door, while Lucy followed.

The image on the card had left Mina with the impression that there might be a ballroom swirling with exotic couples, all engaged in a furiously erotic tango, but the whole building seemed silent, insulated from the unceasing noise of the capital; the room in which Mina now found herself was actually a bedroom.

My God! Mina thought, as she contemplated the king-sized four-poster with the red velvet curtains. *It's not a night club at all. It's a knocking-shop for chubby-chasers!*

59

So far as she was concerned, chubby-chasers were creatures of legend, one of whom she had always longed to meet. Like unicorns, which refused to have anything to do with anyone but virgins, men who were sexually attracted to fat women were exceedingly thin on the ground in Ealing. Then Mina remembered Lucy, who was only half the woman now that she had been as a teenager, and realized that there must be more to the situation than had yet met her eye. She turned, opening her fearful eyes sufficiently to demand an explanation.

"It's all right, Mina," Lucy said. "There's nothing to be afraid of. No one's going to do anything to you that you don't want them to do. But the time has come for you to ask yourself the question: *do I sincerely want to be thin?*"

Mina swallowed a hysterical laugh. The consequent frog in her throat made it impossible to do anything but croak: "Yes."

It seemed a pitifully feeble expression of her desire, but Lucy seemed satisfied. "Good," she said. "I'll cut to the chase, then—no point in beating about the bush. Marcian and Szandor are vampires. Given a few months of weekly sessions, they can literally drink your superfluous flesh away. You'll need to take iron tablets to facilitate the manufacture of new blood, but their enzymes will do the rest—reorientate your metabolism to convert your adipose deposits, that kind of thing. It won't make you feel bad—quite the reverse. You'll feel better than you've ever felt before: full of energy, in more ways than one. Natural selection is a wonderful thing, and we talked only this morning about the marvelous ability of human beings to adapt themselves.

"Marcian and Szandor are human too, of course—you'll have to forget all that superstitious nonsense about the undead rising from their graves and canine teeth becoming fangs. Vampires are just another natural species, near relatives of ours in the genus *Homo*, who accompanied us to the brink of extinction more than once, but are now on the increase again. They're not quite ready to come out of hiding yet—like us, they're not entirely free of their old instincts—but they're making discreet diplomatic moves at every level, taking one step at a time in the tedious business of winning hearts and minds."

Mina hadn't noticed Lucy Stanwere's cliché-addiction before, but she tried to concentrate her attention on the more important aspects of the speech. Apparently, she wasn't going to be required to dance the tango in any literal sense. Instead, she was going to lie down on the bed while Marcian and Szandor drank her blood, presumably relieving her of forty fluid ounces or so, while pumping some kind of enzymes into her that would retune her metabolism to mobilize her fat reserves and set her on the road to paradise, or at least size twelve.

All in all, it was difficult to see a downside.

Eyes wide open now, Mina found herself staring at Lucy's neck, looking for tell-tale holes.

Lucy smiled. "That stuff about fangs is just Hammer horror," Lucy said. "It's more sucking than biting, actually. It doesn't even leave a love bite, because there are no leftovers. You'll feel a slight numbness for a day or two, and your complexion might be a trifle pale, but you'll feel a lot better in yourself."

Mina belatedly thought of a potential downside. "Will I turn into a vampire too?" she asked, surprised at the lack of faintness in her own voice.

"No, silly," Lucy replied. "I told you, they're just another human species. You can't turn into one of them any more than they can turn into wolves or bats. It's symbiosis. They obtain sustenance from us; we get fitness and an amazing sense of well-being in return. Mutual profit—the ultimate expression of free-market economics at its finest. There's no rush; you can have all the time you need to think about it. All we ask is a little discretion."

"Discretion?" Mina echoed, with a confidence she had never felt before. "To hell with discretion. Let's get on with it!"

* * * * * * *

IN THE NEXT two hours Mina discovered why the After Dark Club's card depicted two dancing figures. The movement was internal and emotional, and there were three people involved rather than two, but it was rhythmic as well as hectic, measured as well as erotic.

Marcian and Szandor never touched her below the waist, but that didn't matter. Mina understood well enough, by the time she went to catch the night bus back to Ealing, why sophisticated people said that the most important sexual organ was the brain.

She didn't see Lucy Stanwere before she left. Presumably, that wonderful woman and perfect friend was still engaged in a languorous horizontal tarantella of her own, probably with a single partner given that she no longer had the stored-up wealth to satisfy two. Marcian saw her to the door, bid her a fond goodnight, and made another date with her for the following Tuesday.

The old Mina would have asked, anxiously, whether she'd be ready for another session quite so soon, but the new Mina took it for granted that she could raise her blood to the required pressure with time to spare.

Marcian's conversation had been mostly devoted to technical matters and mild warnings, so Mina felt that he hadn't really warmed to her as yet, but Szandor—who had been silent apart from a few incomprehensible mumblings—had been free to indulge himself in fond stares and tactile explorations, and Mina felt that they had already built a delicate rapport. Although she was besotted with them both, she couldn't help feeling a little fonder of Szandor.

They seemed such nice young men, so expert in their arcane art, that she would have been more than happy to see them again even if the pounds hadn't started to melt away with such awesome rapidity.

It wasn't until the Tuesday, when Mina plucked up enough nerve to make a feeble joke about Dracula, that she discovered how old the seemingly young men actually were.

"Old Vlad!" Marcian said, with a delighted chuckle that was a fine compliment to her joke. "I remember him. Not one of us, of course, just a—how do you say?—*groupie*. Thought he might become immortal if we would only teach him the trick. Poor sap!"

Her experience was so ecstatic that it took Mina ten minutes to realize that she too was a groupie: someone who hung around vampires, avidly offering blood. Twenty more were required to disclose that "poor sap" wasn't an Americanism. "Sap" was a vampire colloquialism for *Homo sapiens*; Marcian referred to his own kind as "ultras"—that being a contraction of *Homo ultrasapiens*, which, loosely translated, meant "man the extremely wise". It wasn't until it was nearly time to go home that it occurred to Mina to wonder how old Marcian actually was, given that he had obviously been around for centuries, but it didn't seem polite to ask forthrightly. After all, he'd been polite enough not to ask *her* age. She resolved to make discreet and indirect inquiries on the following Sunday, for which they made a third date.

By the time Friday night arrived, eight days after Mina's introduction to the joys of vampire victimhood, she felt that her life had undergone a fabulous transformation. As she said good night to Lucy Stanwere she gloried in the conspiratorial glance that they exchanged—a pleasure in which she had never indulged with any other colleague, of either sex, during her entire career in public finance. At work, of course, they behaved with strict formality, never making the slightest mention of their secret, but as they stepped over the threshold each evening they made their silent acknowledgements.

Mina went straight from work to the gym, where she went to work, first on the rowing machine and then on the cycling machine. She sometimes caught other people staring at her, but that didn't make her feel self-conscious any more. Once, they would merely have been appalled by her bulk; now she was content to assume that they were amazed at her capacity for exercise. Regenerating the blood she required to feed Marcian and Szandor was no mere matter of stuffing herself with calories and iron tablets; she had to crank up her retuned metabolism, rebalancing the energy-economy of her physical and spiritual being. Even fake rowing and fake cycling were beginning to give her a sense of furious speed and steadfast endurance that was remarkably satisfying—though not, of course, anywhere near as satisfying as lying on the curtained four-poster while Marcian and Szandor sucked their sustenance from her flesh with such obvious avidity and appreciation.

On Sunday, she observed that it must have been hard for vampires living through times of plague, famine and religious persecution.

"The Black Death was bad," Marcian admitted, "but the Church wasn't too inconvenient. Bishops grow as fat as members of any other priviligentsia. Civilization is a fine thing; life was harder before there were cities."

"You must have very good memories to recall a time when there wasn't," Mina suggested, delicately.

"Ach, it's more tradition than memory," Marcian admitted. "We make up stories to remind ourselves of all the things we're bound to forget. We all feel nostalgic about the good old days before you saps wiped out the Neanderthals, but it's legend-based. Nobody really *remembers* anything much before the fall of Troy, and it's all momentary flashes until the last two hundred years or so."

"The price of living forever, I suppose," Mina said, pensively.

Marcian actually raised his head then, to look her in the eye—as fondly as Szandor, but also a trifle darkly.

"Nobody lives forever, Mina," he said. "Ultras don't age or suffer from disease, but we all die in the end: drowned or decapitated, burned or blown up. *Every* living thing dies."

* * * * * * *

IN THE EARLY hours of that Monday morning Mina stepped on the scales to find that she had broken fifteen-seven for the first time in three years, going in the right direction. She couldn't expect to continue to shed weight at more than a pound a day for very long, of course, but even as the rate of loss tailed off she could reasonably expect to be below fourteen stone by the end of April and below twelve by the end of June. Come Hallowe'en, she might be the woman of her dreams, not an ounce over nine stone and fit as a flea.

Mina had rarely contemplated the future in any frame of mind but abject horror, but she found herself wondering now about very serious questions. When, for instance, would she no longer be able to feed two hungry vampires? Would she have to choose between Marcian and Szandor, or would they settle her fate between themselves? And what, then, would be her long-term prospects? How long could a sap continue to feed a single vampire, if she made every possible effort to maximize her blood-production? Years? Decades? A whole sap lifetime?

Marcian would have known all the answers, but Mina felt that she needed a different perspective. One Friday when she wasn't due at the After Dark, she asked Lucy Stanwere if they could meet up for a drink. Lucy looked her up and down, as if trying to decide whether Mina had lost sufficient weight to be fit company in a sap-filled wine-bar, but eventually nodded. "Let's have dinner," she said. "Do you know the Arlequino Andante in Marylebone High Street? It's late to make a booking, but they'll let me in if I ring."

Mina didn't know the restaurant. but promised to find it and meet Lucy there at eight.

"I've been meaning to have an in-depth chat to find out you were getting along," Lucy said, when they'd ordered, "but you know how it is. It's obviously working. Happy?"

"Never been happier," Mina agreed. "It's just that I've been wondering about a few things, and I don't like to trouble Marcian with too much chat while he's...drinking."

"Oh, Marcy wouldn't mind. He's a real chatterbox by comparison with my Otto. What is it? The not-going-out-in-daylight business?"

"That too," Mina agreed, although it had not been among the items praying on her mind.

"They don't catch fire and shrivel up or anything Hammery like that," Lucy told her. It's just a matter of ingrained habit. Evolution shaped them as nocturnal hunters, like most other vampiric species—bats, bedbugs, and the like. They could give it up if they wanted to, but they don't."

That prompted Mina to think of another question. "If natural selection gave them such long lives," she said, "why did we poor saps get stuck with seventy years?"

"Why did the chimps get stuck with all that hair and no brains? Small differences in DNA can easily be amplified into big differences of lifestyle. We've outstripped chimps because human babies are born at a relatively early stage of development, so our brains gain from experience as they grow. The older we grow the more benefit we get from that experience, so natural selection favors living longer—but we poor saps never got the benefit of the mutation that freed the ultras from the burden of ageing. The corollary is that they reproduce very slowly—ultra males and females don't mix much and only have sex once or twice a millennium—and there's the nutritional limitation too. It has to be human blood, you see—no other species will do. It's almost as if they were our *extra selves*, formed entirely from our spare flesh—but maybe that's a bit too philosophical. The Parma ham's good, isn't it? Nice texture."

Mina found the ham a trifle chewy, and it had a tendency to stick to her teeth, so it wasn't until she was tucking into her veal Marsala that she raised the question of where her new relationship might be headed, medium-term-wise.

"Didn't Marcy tell you?" Lucy asked. "You only had to ask. Szandor will take you on eventually—I hope that's not a disappointing prospect. His English is improving, I hope? He's supposed to be doing night-classes as the City Lit. Marcy runs the Club—he's the fixer for the entire London community. He'll put you on home visits soon if that's okay—just Szandor, I suppose, although Marcy might drop in occasionally. He kept tabs on me for a while, once he'd set me up with Otto. I love Otto. Good job we no longer live in an era when lifelong spinsters were automatically assumed to be consorting with the devil, isn't it?"

"Yes it is," Mina agreed. "When you say *lifelong*...?"

"Don't worry about that," Lucy said. "It's not really a matter of living fast, dying young, and leaving a beautiful corpse. What if we do get used up by fifty or fifty-five? We'll look as good as we possibly can until then, and all you'll ever have to do to reconcile yourself to it is consider the alternative."

Even the new Mina didn't quite have courage enough to ask exactly how old Lucy really was, although she had concluded that appearances were probably deceptive and that Lucy's CV might not be honest about such details as date of birth. It didn't seem to matter much; the crucial datum, so far as Mina was concerned, was her own age, which was thirty-three. If feeding a vampire meant that she was likely to die at fifty-something rather than the contemporary female average of seventy-nine, that didn't seem too high a price to pay for twenty years of better-than-normal slenderness. Anyway,

65

who could tell how many years of life-expectancy her obesity might have cost her if she'd stayed on the boom-and-bust diet carousel?

Mina did, however, summon enough courage to ask whether Lucy had sap boyfriends as well as Otto.

"I had a few, when I still wanted to catch up on all the sex I thought I'd missed out on," Lucy admitted, frankly. "It didn't take long to realize that I hadn't missed anything at all, compared to the *real thing*. You'll find that out for yourself, I dare say."

* * * * * * *

MINA DID FIND out for herself. Indeed, everything transpired as Lucy had prophesied. Szandor's English improved enough for him to ask her himself whether he might visit her at home, once a week to begin with, and Mina readily agreed. Marcian dropped in on her too, once a month or so, more for a chat than a feed. On one such occasion, in August, he mentioned to her that the club had moved, but he didn't give her a card with the new address. Soon after that, Lucy announced that she was moving on again too, having been promoted to a senior position in Newcastle.

Mina breezed through the interview panel for Lucy's job, so the farewell party was a double celebration. It got so wild by midnight that some jumped-up office-boy from Procurement blurted out the office rumor which held that Mina and Lucy were lesbian lovers. Far from feeling appalled or insulted, Mina was delighted that she should be thought so versatile, so desirable and so interesting. She told Szandor about it when he visited her on the following Sunday—Sundays having now become their regular date—but he didn't laugh. It wasn't that vampires didn't have a sense of humor, just that they found different things amusing.

"Anyway," Mina said, "the promotion will mean a hike in salary, so I'll be able to buy a house. You could move in if you wanted to—it might be more convenient."

He laughed at that. "Sank you very much," he said, "but it vouldn't be right."

"Where do you live now?" she asked, for the first time. "Do you have a job of your own—night security or something."

Szandor's gaze, though still fond, became troubled. "I cannot tell you vere I liff," he said. "As for jops, ve liff as ve liffed in the old country, as communists—real communists, not those Soffiet bastards. Effer since...." He broke off.

"Ever since what?" Mina prompted, assuming he was thinking about something that had happened after the collapse of communism, in Bosnia or Chechnya or wherever he had recently come from.

"Effer since the Stone Age," he said. "Ven you began to vork in bronze...ve vere neffer a part of that. The vorld of vork, of jops...is not ours."

Mina realized then how little she actually knew about the vampire way of life, and how they occupied themselves when they were not feeding. She realized, too, how wide the gulf between the two human species must be, if all of history since the end of the Stone Age had been sap history, never recognizing, let alone involving the ultras—except as myth and shadow, mystery and threat. And yet, the ultras lived in a world that saps had remade, an ecosphere that saps had spoiled, on the edges of a global civilization organized and driven by sap machines and money.

Mina nearly asked Szandor what the communist vampires did for money, but realized that she didn't have to. They obtained their money as they obtained their blood, from their sapient groupies—not, evidently, in weekly handouts, but at intervals nevertheless adequate to their peculiar needs. In all probability, they were content to wait until their victims were used up; who else, after all, but her one and only dependent was a groupie likely to appoint as her heir?

Vampires could afford to be patient, and had certainly had abundant opportunity to acquire the habit.

How many victims, Mina wondered, had Szandor had before her? Far more, she guessed, than she had had hot dinners of her own...that being, at the end of the day, exactly what she was. It wouldn't be right for him to move in with her, she realized, for exactly the same reasons that it wouldn't be right for her to move into a battery cage or a veal crate. She was no longer the fat cow she had been in spring, but she would be a cow for as long as she might live.

After that reverie there was only one question that she needed to ask.

"Szandor," she said, "do you love me? Do you *really* love me?"

The ultra paused in his appreciation of the wonderfully appetizing blood that he was sucking from her breast to say: "Yes, my darlink. I loff you ferry much."

Mina knew that it was true. He loved her, not as a child is obliged to love the mother at whose teat it sucks, nor as a farmer is obliged love his prize cattle, nor as saps were obliged by their carefully-selected hormones to love one another, but freely. He loved her in his own unique way, as only a vampire could love a member of his sister species, who provided the substance of his life in a single miraculous red stream.

* * * * * * *

WHEN HER LOVER had gone, after kissing her hand as any overpolite European might have done in saying *au revoir*, Mina went to the full-length mirror that she had brought only the previous day, and stood naked before it to make a critical study of the skin that sagged loosely about her ten stone two pound frame.

There was still a way to go, but she was getting there.

The skin would tighten up in time; even at thirty-three she still had enough adaptability to continue tightening its grip on her compacted flesh.

She would never reach perfection, but every day, in every way, she was getting better and better—and how many hard-working saps could honestly say that...apart from all the others who were secretly in bed with the real reds?

All in all, she told herself, more in self-congratulation than in a spirit of self-discipline, *it's quite impossible to see a downside.*

THE ORACLE

CAXTON AWOKE TO find the Special Branch men going through his drawers with meticulous efficiency. There was no fuss. They flashed their badges, and told him to get up. They waited while he got dressed, watching him like hawks in case he had any more pills hidden away—they'd already confiscated the bottles they'd found on the bedside table. Then they took him downstairs and thrust him into the back of a black BMW.

No one was around to witness his ignominious departure. He knew that someone given him up, but he had no idea who it might be. He had only been hitting the bookmaker for a couple of weeks, taking out no more than he needed for food and to pay off his connection, but all bookies were paranoid and they probably circulated closed-circuit TV pictures of suspected cheats, so it was as likely to be him as anyone else.

He was still trying to rub the sleep from his eyes when the car pulled out into the traffic, and it wasn't until he felt the thrust of the acceleration that the knowledge that it was over actually took hold. The sudden jolt of nausea made him swallow hard, although the dryness of his mouth made it chokingly difficult. He had always found the moment when awful possibility flipped over into horrible certainty was the most difficult to bear of all *waking* moments.

In a fair world, the pain of such catastrophes would have been exactly counterbalanced by the joy of their converse, but Caxton had always found that the reward of hopeful expectation blossoming into blessed relief was meager by comparison. In the days when he had talked to others of his rare and allegedly-precious kind they had agreed with him. One had quoted Schopenhauer, to the effect that anyone who thought that good and evil were balanced out in the course of the world's affairs should ask himself whether the hawk's joy in the kill could be considered equal to its inevitable counterpart, the death-agony of the mouse.

The doctors and scientists had disagreed, of course, but that was what they were paid to do. Theirs was a paradoxical position, which insisted that they sought the truth only in the observations of others, preserving their objectivity while limiting their sight. They were honor- and salary-bound to refrain from the kind of cynicism that lucid dreamers couldn't possibly avoid.

Caxton knew better than to become angry with himself for drugging himself into unconsciousness the previous evening instead of going fishing in his dreams. Even if he'd caught a glimpse of the arrest, he wouldn't have guessed its significance. It was more than likely that he would have been concentrating far too hard on the horses, and the vexatious business of trying to separate the actual runners from the phantom horses of the apocalypse, to pay any attention at all to warnings of his own impending doom. It wasn't as if such warnings had ever been in short supply.

The plainclothesmen took him to the local police station first, because they had to maintain the fiction that his arrest was a matter of the everyday business of law and order. No matter how unjust or futile his arrest might be, it all had to be done by the book. They made every effort to set his uppers and downers down on the custody sergeant's desk as if the pills were proof of some heinous wrongdoing, but they couldn't fake any serious indignation.

"I need those," Caxton told them, quietly. "I didn't have time to take one before I was arrested. If I don't have a wake-up pill I'll be in no condition to be questioned." They didn't care. It wasn't their job to cross-examine him; they were just the delivery men.

"You won't be here long," the sergeant assured him. The Therapy Centre in Maidenhead will send someone to pick you up within the hour. I'll have to take your belt and shoelaces."

Caxton looked down at the grey laces in his Hi-Tec trainers, wondering whether it would really be possible for a man to hang himself with anything so slim and frayed. He shook his head, but he knelt down meekly enough, and slowly began to unthread the offending objects from the network of plastic loops.

"Way back in the last century," Caxton said, because it was obvious that no one else felt like making conversation, "Adolf Hitler sent the Gestapo out to arrest all the astrologers in Berlin. I can't remember why—maybe just one of those little whims dictators have. Not a single one had his bags packed and ready. We all used to laugh at that back at the Bolton Centre, in the early days—as if it were absolute proof that the astrologers were mere charlatans, who could no more see the future than fly. Did it ever occur to you that if I were actually any use—to the Millennium Commission, to humankind, or even to myself—you wouldn't ever have been able to catch me?"

None of them rose to the bait. They were only following orders. It wasn't their job to question the philosophy of the project or the powers of the Commission. They weren't the Gestapo, though; once he was safely deposited in the cell a uniformed constable brought him some tea in a Styrofoam cup. He felt badly in need of the liquid, but he would have preferred strong black coffee. Caffeine wasn't speed, but it was better than nothing.

"I was never a big winner," Caxton said, as he accepted the gift with as much gratitude as he could muster. "No sixty-six-to-one shots. No clever Yankees. I always moved on after a couple of months, to spread the pain. Mr. Hill and Mr. Ladbroke could have supported a dozen like me and never even noticed."

"Was it worth it?" the young constable asked, lingering by the cell door.

Caxton hadn't been expecting that one. "Worth it?" he echoed, helplessly.

"The kind of life you've had to lead," the policeman said, his bright blue eyes peering through the slit with frank curiosity. "Stumbling around from town to town, trying not to attract attention. Why bother? Why not simply do your duty, like any other honest superman?"

Duty! Caxton let the word echo silently in his aching skull. *Is that what it is?* "I'm not a superman," he muttered, thickly. He meant it. Whatever the Bolton Dream Therapy Centre had made of him, and whatever the Millennium Commission wanted from him, he was morally certain that he was no less a prisoner of fate than anyone else. The only difference was that he could see the nightmarish decorations on the walls that surrounded the narrow realm of human choice. He was better than most at measuring the dimensions of the slit in the solid steel door marked FUTURE, but he was no closer than anyone else to finding the key that would open it from the inside.

"But you did win, didn't you?" the young constable pointed out, extending his hand through the slit to accept the cup Caxton had drained to the dark dregs. "Not millions, maybe—but you did win. You can see into the future."

Caxton shook his head, but he didn't try to explain. That was what everyone thought, and not just because of the way the tabloids had reported the original breakthrough. People assumed that it was all so straightforward. You take the drug, you see the future, you make your fortune reading the race results or the lottery numbers in tomorrow's paper—or you could if there weren't more important things to do, more important things to see: important things on which an honest superman had a moral duty to concentrate, not just for the good of the tax-funded Project but for the good of all mankind.

There was a righteousness about the way the constable closed the slit on him, Caxton thought. Like the world-weary men from Special Branch and the custody sergeant, the young constable thought he fully deserved to be banged up—for life, if necessary. There was a job to be done, a problem to be solved, a world to be saved, and it was his job, his problem, his duty. According to the world, he wasn't Simple Simon Caxton; he was Mighty Joe Hope, lurking at the bottom of Pandora's Box: the world's only ward against the looming cloud of evil that might be a stray asteroid, or a new Great Plague, or World War III, or any damn thing at all that could bring civilization down like a house of cards.

Other people never could or would understand that, whatever power the drug had imported to his ragged, wretched mind, he was still just like them in the only respect that really mattered. No matter how much he learned to see, there was no escape.

Caxton had no idea—and nor did anyone else, so far as he knew—whether the fact that he'd sometimes, albeit very rarely, contrived to falsify his own sibylline prophecies meant that the future really could be shaped to the whims of humankind. Perhaps those particular anticipations had been of a special kind, concerned with matters irrelevant to the grim dictatorship of Destiny.

The fault, dear Brutus, is not in our stars, he quoted, silently, *but in ourselves, that we are underlings. Or maybe not. Maybe this time, I'll get to find out.* He didn't believe it. No first-rate miracles had been worked in Bolton; he didn't have the least inkling that Maidenhead would be any different. All he could feel was the horrid insistence of a galloping future that had nothing in it for him but the prospect of being trampled and torn apart. His lucid dreams were government property again, until the day came when the oh-so-lucid nightmares ate up his mind entirely and condemned him to oblivion—or until the end of the world, if that were really as imminent as everyone feared.

* * * * * * *

CAXTON EXPECTED HIS first session with the Maidenhead dream doctors to be uncomfortable, but not because he'd dreamed it in advance. It was only logic that told him so: the same faculty of rational calculation that everyone had. He didn't suppose there would be anyone there that he knew but logic and anxiety alike promised him the same old faces, staring at him with hurt and accusative expressions, and voices, plaintively asking him *why*. Rational calculation suggested that they would do their level best to make him feel guilty about his defection, his dereliction of duty—and he couldn't see any reason why they wouldn't succeed.

It turned out, however, that they had decided to use different tactics. Rational calculation had failed him, just as it routinely failed everyone. Why, otherwise, would the Dream Therapy Centres ever have been set up?

There was only one doctor waiting for him when the burly nurse escorted him from his room, and she was anything but intimidating. She was in her mid-twenties, not quite young enough to be his daughter, although he didn't doubt that she was fully qualified. She was also exceptionally pretty, in a tidy sort of way; the powers-that-be had obviously figured that he needed to be seduced back into the fold.

In a way, he'd have preferred them to use tougher tactics; that might have roused him to resentment, and eventually to dissent, maybe so annoyingly as to give him back the capacity to care.

The first thing the doctor did, after introducing herself as Susan Drayling, was to hand him a plastic bottle containing seven pills. The label said that they were valium, but he wasn't quite ready to believe it.

"Do you think I'm stupid?" he said.

"I think you're scared," she countered, "and I think you've every right to be. They're to help you past the withdrawal symptoms, give you time to adjust. We'll monitor your progress very carefully, to make sure that it's safe to put you back on the lucidity-stimulant. When we think it's safe, we'll tell you exactly what we intend to do and how. The principle of informed consent still applies here."

Caxton suppressed a laugh. "I was brought to the Centre in handcuffs," he pointed out. "The guy who brought me from my room looks like an all-in wrestler. Where's the consent in any of it?"

"You did volunteer, in the beginning," she told him. The softness of her voice seemed to Caxton to be carefully calculated and thoroughly professional. "You signed up for the duration. All the Commission wants to do is hold you to the deal you made, and that's all it's entitled to do. Nobody will try to force the stimulant down your throat or sneak it into your food—but we'll do everything we can to persuade you to co-operate. You understand as well as I do how necessary that is, don't you? You understand exactly why we have to ask you to take the risk, and exactly why you ought to agree. You're not stupid, Simon, and you know how good you were. This Centre never found one to match you—nor did Ashford or Haywards Heath."

"If I were any good at all," Caxton said, knowing that the ploy wasn't going to work, "they'd never have caught up with me, would they?"

"Perhaps, subconsciously, you wanted to be caught," Susan Drayling suggested, arching a neatly-shaped eyebrow. "Perhaps you simply recognized the inevitability of it. Those are among the possibilities I'd like to explore, at any rate. The Bolton people were very disappointed when you ran away, of course, but they always saw it as an opportunity as well as a nuisance—an opportunity to cultivate a better understanding of the psychology of precognition. We're doubly glad to have you back, Simon."

She smiled, winningly.

Caxton tried to see the smile for what it was—a professional smile, fully-laden with hypocrisy—but he could feel himself melting under its pressure. He hadn't seen many smiles recently, and none of the ones he had seen had been directed at him.

"I need *real* downers, and uppers too," he told her. "Barbs to suppress the night-visitors, speed to keep me from napping by day. Valium's no use at all."

"No amphetamines or barbiturates," she said. "Those will let you down as gently as I dare; when they're gone, I won't be issuing any more." She must have known that abrupt withdrawal from the amphetamines would cause worse problems than mere valium could solve, even without the complicating factor of the barbiturates he'd been swallowing three and four at a time, but Caxton could see that she wasn't going to help him out.

"This is torture," he complained. "Plain and simple—and it's all for nothing. It's cruel, and it's pointless."

"Are you casting yourself as a witch or a martyr?" she asked, tartly.

"A heretic," Caxton retorted.

She raised a challenging eyebrow. "And what, exactly, is your heresy?"

"I'm a devout Hartmannist," he told her.

Susan Drayling was, of course, perfectly familiar with the so-called Hartmann Conjecture—which suggested that the whole Dream Therapy project has been a stupid, pathetic, misconceived and misguided waste of time—but mention of it only caused her to reinstate her professional smile.

"So you've been keeping up with the literature while you've been on the run," she parried. "That's good. We need you to understand the possibilities, to approach your own experiences in an informed way. I'd like to make sure that we're talking about the same thing, though—would you mind telling me exactly what you understand the Hartmann Conjecture to be?"

Caxton had to concede that she was slick. "I've had to do my reading in public libraries," he said, in a mock-apologetic tone, "so I've only seen the secondary accounts in *New Scientist*—but I flatter myself that I understood the implications of what I was reading better than most. Hartmann accepts that what you call the *lucidity-stimulant* really does equip a significant minority of the test subjects with a limited, if curiously perverse, ability to obtain true knowledge of the future—but he thinks that the universality of the apocalyptic premonitions experienced by the seers shouldn't be taken as proof of the fact that the world really is in terrible danger. He thinks that the desperate and costly attempts currently being made to obtain a clearer picture of the threat are probably futile. He thinks that the visions of the end which trouble the best of us so deeply are simply an amplification of existential *angst*: that our fearful consciousness of the inevitability of our own deaths is being exaggerated by the stimulant, to the extent that our attempts to bring quotidian events into focus are overwhelmed by a sense of personal hopelessness. That's what we mistake for a teasing vision of the impending end of the world."

Susan Drayling waited for a few seconds before replying, as if she couldn't quite decide which strategy would work best on a patient willing and able to deploy words like *quotidian*. In the end, she kept it brutally simple. "Do you think he's right?" she asked.

"I don't know," Caxton replied, with bitter honesty. "It seems to me, trying to sort through my most recent nightmares, that I'm fucked either way. Whether the dread is purely mine or the whole world's, it's driving me down so hard that I can't get up again. You probably know better than I do what my physical condition is, but if you're going to tell me that there's nothing actually wrong with me I'm not going to believe you. The more terrifying dream-sleep becomes and the more urgent its omens are, the less I can do when I wake—and I can't see any way back. You're right, Doctor Drayling, about my being able to understand how much it matters to you to be able to figure out whether people like me are really seeing the end of the world or merely falling under the spell of our own idiot paranoia—but I hope you can understand when I tell you that if you're so fucking desperate to figure it out you ought to do it the hard way. Why waste time chasing lapsed volunteers when you can replace them so easily simply by volunteering yourself?"

"As a matter of fact," she said, mildly, "two of the research-workers who were working with you in Bolton before you decided to take your little holiday did exactly that. Peter Morden never got past the first round of tests but Janice Carlyle showed better-than-average sensitivity. She's doing well—but someone has to stay on the other side of the needle, Simon. Someone has to observe, to ana-lyze, to weigh things up objectively. Even if the likelihood that the threat is real were far more remote than it is, we'd still have to main-tain the investigation. While there's a possibility that the world really is facing an apocalyptic threat, and a possibility, however slim, that people like you and Janice might be able to figure out when and how, in time for us to save lives, we have to keep the pro-ject going."

"What do *you* believe, Doctor Drayling?" Caxton wanted to know. "Do you believe that it's worth driving people out of their minds, in the faint hope that they might be able to tell you some-thing useful about a threat that might not actually be real at all?"

"I'm a scientist," she said. "My role is to set aside the tempta-tions of belief, to read the facts without prejudice, to try to figure out the truth."

Caxton finally condescended to pick up the bottle of pills that she'd set down in front of him.

"The truth," he said, "is that I can't help you. The truth is that I can't even help myself. I've had all the stimulation I can take, and then some."

"I can't accept that" said the tidy, porcelain-pretty woman who wasn't quite young enough to be his daughter.

"I know," he murmured. That was his problem. He knew that certain things were simply inescapable. Sleep was one of them, and dreams were another—and since the drug had turned him into what-ever he now was, the memory of his dreams was inescapable too.

* * * * * * *

HE TOOK TWO valium tablets that evening, but they didn't help calm his frayed nerves, which were already giving him hell. The only good effect of having to come off the uppers was that sleep was out of the question, tranquillizers or no tranquillizers—but he's learned long ago that you didn't actually have to fall asleep to experience delirium, and that delirium carried its fair share of what modern scientists had chosen to call *lucidity*.

Every time the delirium came upon him he tried to snatch himself wake, but every time he snatched himself awake he only set himself up for the next lapse.

It did no good to look away from the horses, even though he knew that he couldn't use any names they might whisper in his ear. Concentrating on *anything but* the horses was, in the final analysis, exactly the same as concentrating on the horses, except that his imbecilically lucid mind dressed the warnings up in other symbols. He knew all the while that they were only symbols, not real rains of fire or opening abysses or tidal waves or screaming, panicking crowds, but that didn't make them easier to bear. Somewhere among that dreadful crowd of symbols there were items of crude literality, mere brute facts of one kind and another, which could even be seen for what they were once now and again. They might be deceptive in themselves, or siren songs which led him to error, but it did no good to increase his efforts to sort out fact from fiction. Whenever he tried that, the images became so much more clamorous, so much more agonizing, so much more terrifying that the only thing he was capable of wanting, more powerful than the desire to live, was that it should all be fantasy, all unreal, all a mere delusion....

Unfortunately, he thought, as he roused himself for the fifth or sixth time, and almost immediately felt himself relapsing into the same victimized state, he had told Susan Drayling the truth. However much it mattered to her, it didn't actually matter a damn to him whether it was fantasy or not.

The dream-episodes grew worse as the night went on. He found himself insisting, with absurd urgency, that the pit of fire had never opened up beneath Sodom and Gomorrah, that the asteroid had never blasted the dinosaurs to extinction, and there had never been any such things as death camps, or nuclear winters, or mad dictators, or hydrogen bombs, or plague wars, or alien invasions, and that the sun had never exploded at all, or even ignited in the first place....

He tried with all his might to concentrate on the most trivial thing he could find or imagine, even though there wasn't any point in doing that any more, now that he wasn't free to place a bet. It didn't work. Now that he was locked up with his dreams and his duty, and had nothing to do with himself or his life but put the two together and face the horror, he could find no relief in trying to sort out the real horses from those ridden by the horsemen of the Apocalypse.

By the time dawn arrived, he was convinced that the sickness eating away at his bowels like cancer actually was cancer—and that even if it wasn't, it was something else that would neither let him rest nor live, and would show no mercy to him, or to anyone at all, or even any*thing* at all, while it ate up space and time themselves and all the meaning that was in them.

Like acid or the alkahest, irresistible in a universe in which immovability was inconceivable—a universe that had been given over to many-numbered beasts with thousands of heads, in which there would be no more sea or anything at all—the symptoms of his withdrawal ate away at his soul, corrupting everything it dissolved.

He wished that he were a martyr, instead of a devout and committed heretic, so that he might have something to suffer for.

* * * * * * *

CAXTON HAD ALWAYS had nightmares, of course. That was what had made him volunteer for the project in the first place.

He had never been under the delusion that the drugs they gave him at the Bolton Centre would make the nightmares go away—his consent had been informed at least to that extent—but he'd been foolish enough to think that making them more focused by making the dreaming process more lucid might be the next best thing.

He'd even been quixotic enough, then, to think that, if something good could be made to come out of his nightmares, all the distress they'd caused him in childhood might somehow become worthwhile. At first, he really had been prepared to accept martyrdom.

Now, looking back with a sensibility educated by the likes of Susan Drayling, he could see that really—not even subconsciously—he'd just been trying to get back at his father. Mum had always been sympathetic, but Dad had considered it his parental duty to "nip the problem in the bud". Dad had told him to shut up about his bloody nightmares, because they were only bloody dreams and he'd have to bloody live with them like everybloodybody else. Whenever he hadn't shut up quickly enough, Dad had been more than ready to reinforce the lesson with a smack in the head.

Caxton had learned quickly enough to keep his mouth shut, but he'd never learned to forgive. Now, he wondered whether Dad might have had to learn to live with nightmares of his own; nightmares that obviously hadn't given him the ability to pick winning horses but might well have been instrumental in giving him the mother of all bad tempers.

Oddly enough, Jack Caxton had never realized the irony of the fact that his favorite word was "bloody."

On the second day of his new imprisonment, the distressed Caxton confided all of this to Susan Drayling. He had no reason to keep it secret, and he figured that she might well be interested to hear it, but his real reason for doing so was the hope that it might win him some sympathy, and maybe a pill with a bit more clout than the three valium tablets he still had in reserve. He'd taken another two with his breakfast, unable to face the day without them.

It didn't work, of course, but he felt that he had to try.

"Pity the old bastard died so young," Caxton observed. "He'd probably be a lot better at this than I'm supposed to be. On the other hand, maybe the bloody stimulant would have blown that dodgy vessel in his brain as soon as it got into his bloodstream. How many of the people who've died while taking the drug have gone the same way he did?"

"The lucidity-stimulant did increase the risk of cerebral hemorrhage in the early days," Susan Drayling admitted, too neat in her habits to tell an easy lie, "but the beta-blockers seem to have taken care of it. You don't have to be afraid of strokes, Simon. Once you've kicked the bad stuff, we'll give you the medication you really need."

"That all depends what you mean by *have to be* and *really need*, Doctor Drayling," Caxton told her. "There's a sense in which Dad *didn't have to be* afraid of anything, but it was precisely for that reason that the fear he couldn't ever shake off made him hate himself—and everybody else. As to deciding what he *really needed*, I don't think beta-blockers would have been on his list or mine"

"But you're not like your father, Simon," she pointed out, as any shrink would have been bound to do. "You're different. You see more clearly than he ever did—more clearly than he ever could have done. You've never turned your anxieties into violence. You can control it. You can focus. It's just a matter of choosing to focus on something a little less trivial than the racing results. We can help you, Simon—we've learned quite a lot since you went off on your little spree."

"So have I," Caxton said, gritting his teeth. "And the most vital thing I've learned is that triviality is good—and not just because it pays a dividend at the bookies. That's the least of it, Doctor Drayling. Believe me, trivial is best. There are some things that man was never meant to bring into focus."

"You don't believe that," she retorted. "You're too intelligent. But I'd be very interested to hear about your private experiments, so that I could make up my own mind about what there might be to be learned from them."

"I don't like to talk about it," Caxton said. "When I talk about those sorts of thing I think about them too, and when I start think I start having bad dreams. Being here isn't good for me, Doctor Drayling. Just being here is making things worse, even without the uppers and the downers, and the more you make me talk, the worse it will get. You're killing me, Doctor Drayling. You don't even need to stick me with the kind of needle you're itching to use. *This* is enough."

"I think you're over-reacting," she told him, sternly.

"It was my Dad who was over-reacting," he countered, stubbornly. "The ones who over-react are the ones who die and the ones who kill themselves and the ones who simply lose their minds. At the moment, I'm not over-reacting at all—but I don't know how long I can hold on before I start going into overdrive, one way or the other. One hit of the loo-juice is all it would take to make it instantaneous. Believe me, Doctor, I'm burned out as a prophet. You could save my life with the right prescription, but if you don't let me have what I need, I'm gone."

"And yet," she pointed out, "you condescended to be found. Your unconscious screened out news of your own impending capture. After all this time, you let your guard down, and let us bring you back into the program. That was no simple misfortune, Simon. People like you don't experience simple misfortunes. What was it, do you suppose? A death wish?"

"Sometimes," he told her, knowing full well that she already knew it, "we see things clearly but can't lift a finger to prevent them. The dreams are our masters, not our slaves. They don't give us godlike powers, Doctor Drayling—they *are* godlike powers, in their own right. They drive us mad, and they kill us for their sport, and if they don't want the world to be saved they won't ever give us the means to save it. I don't think it matters whether or not I can get past these withdrawal symptoms, Doctor, and I'm absolutely certain that I don't need any more of your fucking stimulant. My mind is all set to blow already, and the only reason the police caught up with me is that there's absolutely nothing left for me to gain by continuing to run. It's over, and I know it. I *know* it—and you can't deny it. I'm the one who can see into the future, after all."

Susan Drayling was studying him very carefully indeed, but not in a way that made him feel like a bug on a microscope slide. She was good at her job, Caxton had to admit, but she wasn't good enough. Nobody was. "Mine eyes have seen the glory of the coming of the Lord," he said, when he realized that she was waiting for him to continue, as if he were merely blowing off steam. "He is trampling out the vintage where the grapes of wrath are stored. Any day now, any way now, I shall be released."

"You wouldn't care to put a date on that, I suppose?" she said, lightly.

Caxton didn't like being humored, but he wasn't about to turn into his father. He made an effort to smile, hoping the result didn't look too contrived. "I'm with Hartmann, remember," he reminded her. "I left Bolton because I couldn't continue to believe—or even to hope—that I was a bit-player in some countdown movie in which the world's most photogenic psychics would come together just in time to stop the sword of Damocles in mid-fall. I don't believe that my nightmares are of any relevance to anyone but myself. I'm no use to you, Doctor Drayling—no use at all."

"If you're scared of cerebral hemorrhage...," she began, speaking very softly and reassuringly.

"Nothing so specific," he countered. "Statistically, of course, suicide is far more likely—anyone who reads *New Scientist* knows that. What did they used to say back in the old days? *While the balance of the mind was disturbed.*"

"But you didn't kill yourself, did you?" she said. "You let them bring you back. That makes you a far better judge than most people as to the best way to utter a cry for help. I think we can help you, Simon. I really do."

"You're wrong," he told her, flatly—but he knew that he couldn't be certain of that. He was confident that he knew himself better than anyone else did, but he also knew that if you doubled next-to-nothing you still wouldn't have very much.

That night he took all three of the remaining capsules, because he knew that one wouldn't be enough and that there was no point in taking two and only holding on to one. They'd be more likely to give him more if he had none at all, if there was any possibility that they'd humor him to that extent. He knew that he was hastening towards his end, but he'd told the simple truth when he told his pretty doctor that the dreams were his master, and that the power they exercised over him was godlike in its irresistibility.

He knew that when he woke up again he'd regret what he'd done, but he was past caring about that. People like him had no alternative but to take each dream as it came.

* * * * * * *

THIS TIME, HE couldn't entirely avoid sleep, but his periods of sleep were no more extended than the periods of waking delirium he'd experienced he night before. The only effect of their being real sleep was to make the periods in between less distinct, more nightmarish in their own right. From time to time he tried to talk himself awake but it didn't work; even talk could be absorbed into the delirium, dissolved into a half-coherent stew of images and ideas.

"Three pills ought to make it earth or water," he chided himself, as resentment sliced his less-than-astral body like a serrated knife, "but if it has to be air and fire it has to be air and fire, and what difference does it make, given that there are far more ways to die than ancient elements—or even modern elements? Every single one of them can fill a crowd with dread and weeping, and you have to concentrate anyhow in the hope of screening something out, even if it means bringing something else into much sharper focus which will be just as bad.

"If you don't try at all, stupid habit will simply take over and you'll see those stupid horses bearing down on you again, with the whip-wielding skeletons laughing like crazy. Even if you don't try to figure out the names they'd tell you names anyway, if only names like War and Plague and Famine and Death, except that this has never been a four-horse race, because that was only ever a brutal simplification, an expression of poetic license employed by dreamers who never understood how lucky they were to *have* a poetic license."

In the past, he knew, dreamers had been so stupid as to wish that they could see more, and see it more lucidly. They hadn't had the opportunity to realize that there was no Hell deeper or more fiery than the Hell of knowledge and lucidity: the Hell of stimulated dreams; the Hell of *knowing* that the End was Nigh, that the Apocalypse was Now, and that the future was even more crowded with ague and anguish than the plaguey present or the petrified past.

"Dreamers of old would have put out their eyes rather than see *this*, or *that*," he muttered, biting his bleeding lips, "or try to put a name to the Thing that was even now reaching out to them, or try to put a time to the moment when the air and fire would seize upon *you*. Dreamers of old never knew how lucky they were not to see the Thing that would rip you apart and squeeze you into a cinder, blow you away and burn you up, and hide its face all the while—and challenge you to try to see it, to try to concentrate, because it knew, just as you knew, and just as every other lucid dreamer in the world had to know, that nothing was or is or ever will be more terrifying than knowledge, than truth, than sleep."

He knew, even as he said it all, that it made no sense and couldn't be true. But he knew, too, that there was truth in his dreaming, that he and those like him really were *the oracle*....

* * * * * * *

"FAIR ENOUGH," SUSAN Drayling replied, equably, as she watched him sweat and squirm with her vilely clinical eye. "Let's leave personal matters aside, by all means. Let's keep it strictly objective, scientific. On the basis of all the publicly available evidence, what do you think is happening, Simon? What kind of apocalypse do you think we're most likely to be facing? *Is* it the *Book of Revelations*, or something science fiction?"

It was more trailing bait. *Just forget your dreams and focus on the evidence.* As if!

"It's definitely something science fiction," Caxton said, with all the sarcasm he could muster from the raiment of his distress. "Back in the days of Saint John, the collective unconscious was way too strong to let the celestial dreamers through. Everyone was a psychic island in those days. It's only within the last hundred years that the walls of darkness have been properly breached. The celestial dreamers aren't doing it on purpose, of course—they're just the innocent alien inhabitants of all the worlds of all the stars, locked into their blissful communion. If they were ever individuals they lost their individuality aeons ago, just as we'll lose ours. I can't put a date on it because it won't happen all at once. I could go tomorrow or the day after, but you'll probably last ten or twenty years, maybe thirty. You'll probably outlast the infrastructure of society and all its desperate excrescences: the MC, the Samaritans, the DTCs, His Majesty's Government, the UN, the Churches. The very last thing you'll learn is that you can't change a thing. Believe me, Doctor Susan Drayling. I know."

She nodded gravely, as if she'd learned a lot instead of sweet fuck all—as if he were talking sense instead of arrant nonsense. That was the trouble with shrinks, he thought. They tolerated far too much.

She pointed at the empty bottle in his hand and said: "You were only supposed to take one last night and one this morning. We trusted you to do that."

"If you simply wanted to wean me off them you'd have doled them out two by two, then one by one," Simon countered, knowing that he was right. "You gave me seven at once to make a point—and to shift the blame. This way, you get me off them all he sooner and you get to make out that it's all my fault. If you weren't desperate, you wouldn't be resorting to games like that."

"We do feel a certain sense of urgency," she admitted. "Don't you?"

"Believe me, Doctor Drayling," he said, wishing that he could muster a flicker of lust at the sight of her, or a flicker of anything but gut-wrenching nausea, "you haven't the slightest idea what a *sense of urgency* is."

"If you can give us more," she said, "we'll consider giving you more valium. One at a time, to begin with—two if you can give us something good, something solid."

"From anyone but a fully-qualified doctor," Caxton observed, sickly, "that would sound like crude blackmail."

"What choice have we got?" she said.

"What choice does any of us have?" he countered. He knew that his tactics were at fault. He knew that he ought to pretend to be co-operative. He knew that he ought to feed her something that looked solid, that looked good. He knew that he ought to try to string her along, play the game the only way it could be played—but knowing wasn't enough. Even when knowing was too much, it wasn't enough.

"And if I don't come through tomorrow," he said, not couching it as a question, "you'll start giving me the stuff again. Even though you know it will kill me, one way or another."

"We don't want to harm you," she said. It was true, but it wasn't enough. Even when the truth was too much, it wasn't enough. She had the dose all ready; he knew that she'd have the needle in his arm right now if the case conference had decided that it was the way to go. She was just a puppet, like him—a puppet dancing to a tune she couldn't hum.

"If I could help you," he said, truthfully, "I would."

"We'll talk again tomorrow," she promised. "You really do have to get past this awful shakiness. One way or another, you have to get through it, and we can't just keep filling you up with valium. We really do want you to get well, so that you can get back into the program. Tomorrow, you'll feel better. I'm sure you'll make more sense when you do."

Caxton didn't know whether that was true or not, and the fact that he didn't know was almost as terrifying as the knowledge would have been—and the only thing more terrifying than that was the awful inevitability of sleep.

* * * * * * *

84

WHEN NIGHT FINALLY fell, after an absurdly long and troubled time, Caxton didn't try very hard to fight the awful inevitability of sleep. He continued to look at the TV, although he wasn't capable of actually watching it, until two in the morning, but that was as far as he could go.

He had heard of people in situations not unlike his who had punched the wall for hours on end, people who had ripped gasping wounds in their own flesh, but he had never heard of anyone who'd stayed awake forever and he had heard of people who'd begun to dream continuously and inescapably anyway, just as lucidly as they would have done had they actually fallen asleep.

Without the killing power of the barbiturates, without even the futile soothing of the valium, he was lost. It was as simple as that. The power of the pills was killing power. The dreams were alive: alien visitations requiring the intervention of a bug-exterminator. In the beginning, Caxton had wondered whether they might somehow be domesticated—tamed as pets or confined as battery hens—but he was sure now that they were irredeemably wild, that they never would lay their nuggets of information regularly and cleanly. In an ideal world, he'd be able to get up every morning at the same hour as normal people, with all the day's racing results neatly filed away and nothing horrible to confuse them—but in an ideal world the universe of stars wouldn't be filled with alien dreamers whose insidious assaults were gradually breaking through the protective walls of the human collective unconscious, destroying the souls that made people into people instead of anonymous molecules of mind in the great undifferentiated ocean of the Cosmic Mind.

Not that I really believe any of that crap, he told himself, as he lay in the dark, staring into nothingness, *any more than I believe that the last trump is about to sound, so that the dead might rise from their graves and form an orderly queue before the Seat of Judgment. It's all fantasy, invented in the hope of making sense of the nonsensical, explaining the inexplicable, making the unthinkable thinkable.*

Eventually, no matter that he had no barbs to help him, he drifted off to sleep. The only difference was that he couldn't avoid he dangerous layers and dive straight into oblivion. Instead, he was eerily half-conscious of the whole process: every sliding step of it. He felt and saw the oracular dreams arrive to claim him

He dreamed, as he always had, of terror.

That was, at the end of the day, the whole of it. What he saw didn't really matter at all, even the tiny fraction of what he saw that was potentially capable of refinement into fleeting glimpses of the facts of the future. All that mattered, really, was what he *felt*—because he was, in essence, and like every other human on Earth a man of feeling.

What he felt was terror, pure and simple.

All that the future had ever held, beyond the few fugitive glimpses that had provided him with his perversely precarious and conscientiously marginal living, was the threat of extinction. Given that, what else mattered? Given that, what was the point of confining him, of trying every means that existed, fair or foul, in the stupid and utterly vain hope that there might be something lurking at the bottom of his private Pandora's Box that could cancel out all the overlaying hosts of troubles?

He slept, but he slept badly—and he knew that it could only get worse. He knew, too, that the doctors would do everything they could to prevent him from killing himself—and he knew that they might succeed.

* * * * * * *

IN HIS NEXT session with Susan Drayling he answered all her questions truthfully, on the assumption that if his nights were doomed to get worse and worse he might as well do what he could to make his days as easy as possible. He gave her a list of winning horses, but he warned her not to start playing the Oedipus game.

"You can ring up all the trainers and instruct them to withdraw the runners," he told her, "or you can have the bloody things shot as they come round the final bend, just to prove that destiny isn't implacable—but if you do that, I'm a vegetable. Anything you alter rebounds on me; anything substantial will set off a bomb in my brain. *Et tu, Brute*."

"That's not what you said before," Doctor Drayling pointed out. "You said that nothing could be changed."

"I said that I couldn't change anything, and that you couldn't either. Bomb-blasts aren't selective, Dr. Drayling. Take my advice—if you want to be here tomorrow, make sure that what will be will be. Bet by all means, but bet modestly. I suppose you know how I killed my father?"

"I know how you think you killed him," she admitted. "It was a stroke like any other stroke. It might not have been the fact that he was trying to prevent your vision coming true. It could have been a coincidence."

"So could the winning horses. So could everything that persuaded the Millennium Commission to take precognition seriously.

If you doubt me, all you have to do is try to make sure that one of those horses doesn't get to post."

She put the list away in a drawer.

"We don't want to hurt you," she said, by way of reassurance rather than threat, "but we have to do everything we can to make use of your ability. We can't just sit back and let the world end without trying to prevent it, can we?" Her last comment was almost plaintive. Caxton saw that she knew full well that she was playing with fire. She knew full well that she was playing with *the* Fire.

"There's nothing you can do," he told her—honestly, so far as he knew. "There are only two ways to live in these Last Days: in hope or in terror. I don't have the choice, but you do. Be glad that you're blind, Dr. Drayling."

"I can't give up," she told him. "We can't give up. We have to try, and we have to force you to help us. You do understand that, don't you?"

"Of course I do," he retorted. "Why do you think I've lived my life the way I have? Why do you think I'm dying my death the way I am? What other choices have I ever had?"

* * * * * * *

WHEN TWO IN the morning rolled around again Caxton switched off the TV and meekly lay down on his bunk, wondering whether sleep itself might be a defense mechanism. Maybe it was a device thrown up by natural selection to put the dreams in psychic prison, to hold them back from breaking through into waking life and conquering consciousness itself. Maybe the unconscious, regardless of whether Freud or Jung had made the better map of it, was just one of many barbed-wire barriers erected to keep the awful truth at bay. Maybe he had told Susan Drayling the simple truth when he said that it was only in the last hundred years that the barriers had really begun to crumble. Maybe the formulation of the Fermi paradox had been the trigger.

If we are not alone, where the fuck are they?

In Heaven, Enrico. All in Heaven, in blissful union with Creation—and we can't keep them out any longer. No matter how hard we try, the knowledge is forcing itself upon us: the knowledge that destroys the distinction between past and future; the knowledge that nothing is changeable, that everything merely *is*.

He wasn't yet asleep, but he could feel himself trembling. He was sweating again too, but sweating with pure terror rather than any mere physical malaise. There was nothing he could do to deaden himself against it.

If he had been given a pill he would have taken it—or two, or five, or however many he had been given...but he had none, and he knew that he had always been fated to come to this moment having none: that nothing he could have done, even in the full glare of consciousness, could have altered this eventuality, even though it had been the result of a long series of considered and calculatedly perverse choices.

Susan Drayling had rewarded his co-operation by holding back the lucidity-stimulant for one more day, but he knew full well that he no longer needed that kind of help. He was already wide open, and had been since the day he took flight from Bolton.

Even though he was not yet asleep, his stream of consciousness was becoming a deranged shower of images, and he couldn't keep the train of his thoughts together. Terror was in him, as it always had been, and he had no way to fight it—no way at all.

Waking, he dreamed, and he saw, and he was what he saw, and he smiled as he saw that he was right and right and right again, and always had been. He was right because there was nothing he or anyone else could be but right, because there was no other way to turn and no way at all to sin. Everybody, in the end, had to go to Heaven.

Everybody, in a sense—perhaps the only sense that mattered—always had been in Heaven. What would be was as absolute and eternal as what had been. The human race was fixed, like any other race, and every runner was an also-ran, so there wasn't a winning bet on the book. He realized, too, the final cost of living on the margin—of stretching his freedom the only way freedom could be stretched, of staying one step ahead of the *doppelgänger* dogging his every footfall, of staying hidden and being discreet, of being moderate and growing old, of beating the odds and knowing all the while that the odds could never be beaten, of staving off the inevitable until the inevitable became the inevitable because it had always been the inevitable.

He gritted his teeth and squeezed his eyes shut against the pain and the light, the hurt and the enlightenment. Doctor Susan Drayling had no idea at all how little time she had, how little time everybody had.

It wasn't necessary to set a date for the End of the World, or the time of night when the darkness was deepest, because the dawn would never come.

And for the first time in is life, Simple Simon Caxton saw the celestial dreamers clearly, in all their terrifying beauty, and all their horrid harmony, and all their stupid, futile, insane Allness. He knew that it wouldn't have mattered a damn if he'd swallowed a pill, or two, or five, because time was and time is and time will be, and all the time in the world is *never*.

No way in the world was Dad's stroke just a stupid coincidence, he thought, while thought was still possible and still, somehow, seemed desirable. The celestial dreamers themselves burst the vessel in his bloody brain and flooded his bloody brain with bloody blood, and serve the bloody bastard right. When had it ever been any different for Oracles—for those who saw that they could see, and proved to others that they saw what they could see, even though the others couldn't see, and couldn't understand, and couldn't control their stupid, futile hunger to *know*, because they couldn't escape the stupid, futile illusion that if only they *knew* there would be something they could do.

It was, after all, perfectly bloody obvious to anyone with half a bloody brain that if anything could be changed it couldn't be seen and couldn't be known and couldn't even bloody *be*.

But he wondered, when he knew—with a curious sense of relief—that he was well and truly lost, whether it really was THE END for *everyone*, or whether what he had taken for THE END might not be the triumph of the celestial dreamers at all, but simply his own personal end: which could not be contained, but could not, in the end, be or become anything but his own personal nothingness.

He hoped, honestly and sincerely, that it was only his own death that had brought itself about by the terror of foreknowledge. He wished no ill to anybody else. As a devout Hartmannist, he wanted both humanity and reality to endure forever—and perhaps even, in time, to get to know one another a little better.

THE TOUR

THE WORST THING about virtual holidays is climbing into the gel-tank. It always seems to take an age and a half to get the paraphernalia attached. I appreciate that the mouthpiece and all its damned filaments have to be set just right, so that you can get the full benefit of the texture and taste sensations, but I don't understand why there's so much fiddling about down the other end. It's just a matter of piping away the wastes, after all. Then there's that uncomfortable interval, when the hood still feels like a hood and the gel still feels like gel. No matter how expert you become in stepping over the threshold of reality, it still takes time to get fully involved with the Other World.

That's one of the reasons why I always prefer to go on holiday with an organized tour-party. It's much easier to adapt to a virtual world if you're in company, and real company is much better than mere illusion. Maybe that shows a lack of sophistication on my part. Some people think there's no discernible difference between real and illusory companions—after all, your fellow tourists are just computer-generated simulacra whether they're hooked up to real people or not, and it takes a real expert to spot a Turing these days—but it makes a difference to me. I like to know that I'm part of an authentic crowd.

You never know how many of the seats on any particular tour bus they've actually sold, of course, so you never know how many of your fellow travelers are Turings painted in to make up the crowd, but you can always be certain that most of them are real, or they'd have closed the whole operation down. The Divine Comedy tour does have a solo version, and it's easier for the company to cater to one tank at a time. They don't run the group software unless there's a healthy demand.

As it happened, Philly, the only person in my regular chat room who'd taken the tour had done it solo, and he waxed lyrical about it. "To get the full effect," he said, "you have to be Dante. You have to be alone in the wild wood; you have to walk with Virgil one-on-one; you have to see God for yourself. Looking out from behind a wall of glass while you're nibbling canapés with a whole bunch of gawkers would be a totally different thing. It'd be like eating a sweet with the wrapper on."

I hadn't had a reply ready but Jean-Paul was always on hand to chime in. "That's your paradoxical Protestant heritage talking, Philly. If you were a Catholic, like Dante, or a Catholic atheist, like me, you'd realize that faith-fantasy has to be a collective thing. The whole point is that we're all in it together."

"Oh sure," Philly came back. "That's why they call the tour bus a gondola, is it? To remind the rubes they're in Catholic country? Calvinism doesn't mean that it's just every man for himself and God, you oaf—it means that it's the whole community and God without any meddling middlemen. Whatever you call the damn thing, a tour bus is a tour bus—and a gaggle of gawkers is a gaggle of gawkers. Doing the tour in a crowd is an aesthetic atrocity which no sensitive person should even contemplate committing."

When I read that one I thought *Wow!* I wondered if there was a special circle of Hell set aside for committers of aesthetic atrocities—but I left them to argue it out between themselves. I didn't want the experience spoiled by their petty quarrels.

As I see it, it's just a simple fact that some pleasures are best enjoyed in real company. Solitude isn't in short supply, after all. You can slip into your data-suit and plug yourself into a solo trip any day of the week, in the privacy of your own home. If you're going to splash out on something special, you want it to be different. A holiday is a holiday is a holiday—and on any kind of tour, trying to form a rewarding relationship with a passenger of the appropriate sex is at least half the fun. When you get right down to the nitty-gritty, it's all just pantomime—even real life.

Anyhow, it was worth it in the end. By the time they'd finished adjusting the bits and bobs I was raring to go. It only took me a few more minutes to get the observation-deck properly into focus, and by the time I had a champagne-glass in my left hand I was well and truly in. I had to save the right for the introductions. You can't memorize all the names, but you still have to shake their hands and match their ultra-bright smiles—and you can make sure that you remember the names of the most interesting women.

* * * * * * *

YOU ALWAYS GET the brightest smiles of all from the guides. "Hi," said the senior partner, "I'm Virgil. This is Beatrice. Great to have you aboard, Mr. Wheeler. I'm sure you'll enjoy the trip."

"As long as you don't do the commentary in Latin," I said, awkwardly conscious of the fact that they'd probably heard it half a dozen times already.

Virgil laughed anyway. "Any language you like," he assured me, before the two of them moved on to the next handshake.

Virgil and Beatrice were the only persons on the deck guaranteed to be fakes, but least they weren't dressed in togas, and Virgil didn't have a laurel wreath on his head. They were both young, lean, and handsome—just like everyone else, in fact, except that Virgil had a certain indefinable *gravitas* and Beatrice a deftly calculated naivety. Because Turings are exactly what they appear to be, they can be designed to near-perfection. Those of us whose beauty isn't even skin deep tend to be a little less artful in our performances.

I wasn't worried about the language, of course, but I was too polite to voice my hope that the commentary wasn't going to be too heavy. The so-called Angel of the Lord had been a real pain on the Sodom and Gomorrah Experience, and that had only been a day trip. I suppose the researchers have to be seen to earn their paychecks, but I don't see why I should have to suffer.

By the time we'd toasted the launch I'd met everybody, although I hadn't said much more to any one of them than I'd said to Virgil: a hi, a smile and a feeble one-liner. You can't just dive in; you have to study the field.

People on organized tours fall into four categories: the tightly-bound couples whose only interest is in one another, the loosely-bound couples looking to juggle, the singles looking to pair off and the singles looking to rack up a score. Personally, I'm category three looking for other category threes. I used to be a category four when I was as young as I look in VR, but I've grown out of it. It's too messy and too distracting. You have to find a healthy balance between the sights you've actually come to see and interacting with your fellow sightseers. If you can't do that, you might as well be at home hooking up your suit to a porn channel or a contact net. If you're only interested in racking up a score you don't need to go to Hell to do it.

The first candidate I selected for a second conversational shot was a blue-eyed blonde, orthodox without being a thoroughgoing Barbie. I suppose I was lucky to get such an early opportunity—that type usually has an instant honey pot effect, and the look never goes out of fashion—but she'd been carefully cornered by some body-language expert who'd abruptly moved on to a new maneuver and was temporarily at a loose end.

"Hi," I said. "It's Helen, isn't it? I'm Max."

"I remember," she lied. Blue-eyed blondes never bother to make mental notes; they know perfectly well that the burden of expectation is on the other side.

"What do you think of Virgil?" I asked, nodding my head towards the podium. Virgil had already launched into his spiel, although he hadn't exactly riveted our attention yet.

"I don't know," she said. "I just hope he doesn't get too heavy. I don't know very much about Dante or the Renaissance, and the finer points of Church politics are way beyond me."

A twin soul, I thought. "He won't," I assured her. "It's not an educational trip, after all. It's a fun thing."

When I tuned in to what the guide was actually saying, though, I wasn't so sure. Maybe it was just that there wasn't a lot to say about the dark wood and its denizens. Helen seemed disappointed too.

"Who cares what the leopard, the lion and the wolf are supposed to symbolize?" she whispered. "Wouldn't we get more of a kick out of them if they were just scary?"

"But they're not very scary, are they?" I pointed out. "If we were on foot, perhaps...but we're up here. Anyhow, *we*'ve all been on safari. Poor Dante never had the chance. To him, leopards and lions were probably fabulous beasts, like dragons or hippogriffs."

I could tell that she didn't know what a hippogriff was, but she wasn't about to admit it. "He'd have seen them in the Coliseum," she said. "They used to import them to fight gladiators." Either she was overdoing the innocent act or she had no sense of chronology whatsoever.

"I think they stopped importing lions when the Christians took over," I said, playing along in case it was a joke. "Too many bad memories."

I'd done a little homework, so I knew enough to look out for the inscription on the lintel of the doorway into Hell. It was some doorway—but it had to be, if the gondola were to pass comfortably through it.

"Abandon hope all ye who enter here," I quoted, as we passed beneath.

"I preferred the bit about the high wisdom and the primal love," Helen replied. It sounded like encouragement, but her manner was conscientiously distant; we both had a lot of circulating still to do.

By the time we were over the river crossing I'd moved on to Matilda, who was clad entirely in black, from her silken hair to her shiny boots. It's not a look I normally go for, but this was Hell after all.

"Bit of a patchwork so far, isn't it?" I said.

"Day one's always slow," she said, laconically. "It builds up anticipation."

"That scowling ferryman's long overdue for replacement by a bridge," I opined. "It's a good job this so-called gondola's as good in the water as it is on land."

"It's just local colour," she said. According to Virgil, who was still going nineteen to the dozen, it was symbolism again. The great divide between life and death, time as a flowing stream, etc, etc.

"You can have too much symbolism, I always think," I told Matilda, loftily. "If everything in Hell were just symbolic, it wouldn't be Hell at all, would it?"

"Oh, I don't know," she countered, refusing to play the kind of game that Helen took for granted. "It's only the appearances that are symbolic. The pain's still real, isn't it? It'll be the same in Heaven, God willing. However you try to imagine it, it always seems silly—clouds, green fields, choirs of angels—but that's because you can only think about such things in symbolic terms. Behind the pretty picture, though, the joy has to be real."

I didn't like to be outdone, even though I wasn't certain that I could come up with anything clever enough to pass muster. I just pitched in and trusted to luck.

"There are symbols and symbols," I said, airily. "I mean, looked at with a clinical eye, that rabble of nameless souls is just a dust-storm with sound-effects. Sure, it tells us something about the status of the dead in the eyes of the living and the insignificance of the human horde in the eye of cosmic time, but if you're to get the full benefit you have to stop thinking about it as mere symbol and try to see it as if it really were a vast array of actual human spirits, each one of them just like you or me but lost in the wilderness of infinity."

She laughed. There seemed to be genuine delight in the laugh, but I wasn't sure that it was an appropriate response. I'd been aiming for something a little more respectful—but delight is delight, after all, and the laugh wasn't unpromising.

For a while I didn't even try to engage anyone else in conversation. I just stood on the polished boards, sipping my champagne and devouring my smoked salmon, watching the Other World go by. Unfortunately, I'd chosen a bad time to go into reflective mode. Limbo was about as exciting as you'd expect, with all the airy-fairy types making the most of their noble dignity. Unlike our guide, most of these guys were dressed in togas and they were hamming up the philosopher act without an atom of subtlety. Mind you, if I'd had to live in that Disneyland castle for all eternity I'd have found it difficult to crack a smile myself.

This time, I was the one who got buttonholed, and the one who had to pretend to remember a name that hadn't stuck during the whirlwind of handshakes.

"Sophia, of course," I lied. "I remember. I'm Max."

"I know," she said—and might even have been telling the truth. Sophia was far less striking than either Helen or Matilda, but she had poise and a certain air of maturity. People who are old often play young in virtual space, but it rarely works the other way around, so I assumed that she really must be pretty mature—assuming, that is, that she was real at all. Given the unconventional nature of her display, Sophia seemed far less likely to be a Turing than Helen or Matilda, but there's really no way to know how the layers of bluff stack up. At the end of the day, no matter what anyone says, there's no way to tell what kind of person—if any—might be lurking within what kind of appearance. A refined thirty-fiveish slim introvert with kind eyes and a delicate hint of grey in her hair is just as easy to fake as a twenty-two carat Barbie.

"If the Divine Comedy's joke is that we only think this is a holiday," I said, "we're likely to be stuck in Limbo for a long time, aren't we? We're all unbaptized innocents, after all."

"Oh no," she said, with just the right combination of earnestness and wit. "The Church still exists, even though no one pays much attention to it. The creed is available to us, even though no one has faith any more. We've refused it, so we're certainly bound for Hell. If this isn't really a holiday, it's the last part of the tour we'll be missing out on."

"They let Dante into Heaven," I pointed out.

"They also let him out again," she countered. "If we're only fooling ourselves about this being a holiday, we won't be going home, will we? Once we've got to our appropriate places of punishment, we'll be disembarked."

"One by one or all at once?"

"Oh, one by one I should think. We're all sinners, but we haven't all favored the same sins."

"Well," I said, feeling that I was keeping up rather well, "if the others start disappearing when we get to whichever circle fornicators go to, we'd better be careful, hadn't we?"

"I'm always careful," she assured me. "Catch you later."

That was easily the most promising of my preliminary encounters, but I knew better than to jump to any premature conclusions. It was all testing the water, after all. It was difficult to tell which of the three was most likely to be interested in me in the longer term. Hardly anyone goes in for straightforward signaling these days; it takes skill to figure out exactly what kind of script someone is playing to, whether you're responding the way she wants you to, and how you measure up to the opposition. I judged that if Helen was playing "opposites attract" then I might still be a plausible candidate, but not the only one. If Matilda was playing "ships that pass in the night" I might yet be the vessel in question, but it did seem less likely. It was pretty obvious that I'd have to play up to Sophia on a "meeting of minds" basis, but I figured I could do it. Until I'd made a few tentative moves in each direction, though, it would be difficult to figure out what my own personal preference was, let alone where my best chance lay.

I didn't make any serious moves that evening. There was no rush, and first night propositions are always likely to seem crude and hasty. Mature people have to observe better aesthetic standards than a bull in a china shop.

* * * * * * *

MOST PEOPLE SAY they sleep exceptionally well in a gel-tank, but I've never been a deep sleeper. Not that I'm much of a dreamer, mind—or if I am, I'm certainly not one to remember my dreams. When I woke in my virtual bed I felt thoroughly refreshed and ready to face the next Circle of Hell.

The action started with Minos the infernal judge, who was a very respectable horror-movie effect, and went on to the circle of winds where the souls who sinned for lust were tossed hither and yon.

There were plenty of useful conversation-pieces in the circle of the winds—it was a real ice-breaker, probably planned that way by the tour-operators. There's nothing like a bit of storm and stress for making a tour party draw together, acutely aware of their privilege in being safe and warm on the deck of a four-star cruise-vessel. Perhaps the emphasis on the erotic would have been better left to the evening, but if the operators had done that they'd have had to let us languish in Limbo for a lot longer, and that would not have been a good idea.

Once Francesca had done her party-piece it was on to the circle of the gluttons. I suppose the sight of millions of lovers of luxury beaten down by cold and heavy rain isn't remotely exciting in itself, but it made a nice counterpoint to lunch.

"It gives a whole new meaning to the concept of just desserts, doesn't it?" I said to Helen. I wouldn't have risked the line on Matilda, let alone Sophia, but Helen liked it well enough. She mumbled something about profiteroles, which was presumably supposed to be a convoluted play on words, but she hadn't quite finished her last mouthful and it faded away into a mumble.

I was almost tempted to remind myself that we weren't actually eating real food at all—just manna, served up by the mouthpiece according to the regulation diet—but there's no point taking virtual holidays if you keep thinking about what's happening underneath. You have to commit to the illusion.

The sight of the avaricious and the prodigal brawling in the fourth circle got the adrenalin flowing again, although Virgil's lecture on the calculus of probability and its relevance to the calculation of life-chances didn't have nearly enough jokes in it. In the meantime, Helen turned out not to be playing "opposites attract" at all. She wandered off after lunch and by the time we sat down to dinner she was practically glued to an incredibly tedious muscle-bound apparition who was as blatant a forgery as anything I'd ever encountered. It was the sort of beefcake look that had gone out with the twenty-first century, so it was long odds on that the guy using it had to be seventy-five if he was a day—but I'd begun to pick up hints that if Helen was real she was probably of much the same vintage. I switched my attention back to Sophia, figuring that I was ready for a little intellectual banter.

"Watching the wrathful wrestle in mud isn't my idea of fun," I confided to her, "and the fact that the arrogant can't even be bothered to wrestle makes them utterly uninteresting."

"You have to be careful of ready judgments," she said, playfully. "It's often our own particular sins to which we're blindest."

"Maybe so," I told her, "but I know myself pretty well. Wrath isn't my thing at all, and I only go in for arrogance in an ironic sort of way. Lust's more my sort of thing."

"Lust's everyone's sort of thing. Everyone has to say so, at any rate. What would people think of us if we confessed that we had no interest in lust?"

"They'd think we had no business being on this sort of tour," I answered. I knew it was the right answer; it was the kind of question only an idiot would get wrong. We had a good night together; there was nothing wrathful in our wrestling and nothing arrogant in our eventual relaxation. Lust was evidently her sort of thing too, at least for the time being.

"Only a few more infernal regions to go," she murmured, as she drifted off to sleep. "First Malebolge...and then Purgatory."

* * * * * *

THE NEXT MORNING we set off with the Furies in attendance, and soon came within sight of the City of Dis. Virgil told us that he and Dante had had difficulty getting in first time around but that the tour company had managed to negotiate a special deal with the fallen angels. It was nothing but a vast cemetery, of course, but what a cemetery! All those open tombs full of flames—and all for the punishment of heresy, which in this enlightened day and age is so far removed from sinfulness as to be virtually compulsory.

It turned out, though, that my ideas on the subject of heresy weren't entirely to Sophia's taste. Although I'd fully expected us to be cozy all day long and then some, she seemed to have other ideas. I hadn't taken her for any kind of score-chaser, but she certainly seemed to be still looking around. A more sensitive man might have felt unduly anxious about what he might have done wrong, but I just reminded myself that she'd been the one to strike up a conversation with me on day one.

By lunchtime I was back on course with Matilda. As we descended into the real depths of Hell, towards the murderers and the rapists, the frauds and the traitors, I began to feel a real bond of sympathy growing between us.

"This is more like what I expected," I confided to Matilda. "Rivers of boiling blood, fiery rain, deserts of burning sand...."

She took up the refrain without any evident effort. "Demonic centaurs, people turned into trees, hellhounds...sure, Max—this is Hell, nor are we out of it. I don't know about the demons, though, don't they seem to you to be just a bit...well, a bit too Doré."

I'd done just enough homework to know who Doré was. "I rather like the traditional look," I said. "I don't like too much impressionism."

"Almost as bad as too much symbolism, I dare say," she countered—but she wasn't being snide. Even Virgil had given up on symbolism now; in fact, his commentary had become noticeably more relaxed. Most of what we could see spoke for itself, and there was plenty of it.

The pits of Malebolge were so good that the operators were careful not to send us through too fast, and canny enough to save some for the next day.

Matilda and I still hadn't quite got it together, although we were both pretty clear about the direction we were heading. We went to our separate beds, but I was certain that we were both deferring the pleasure for the sake of increasing anticipation. I figured that the person behind the black-clad mask must be one of my own generation, with exactly the right balance of youth and experience.

Day four got off to a flying start, with the demons crowding around the bus as if they were the tourists and we were the side-show. It was wonderful stuff: all those deformed faces peering in, forked tongues licking yellow tusks, gnarled fingers pointing, all those eyes glinting with anticipation.

"Very Doré," I said to Matilda.

"Very, very Doré," she agreed.

Virgil was busy reciting the names of the demons and directing our attention to the occasional head popping up from a river of seething pitch, but this was when we all began to tell one another tales. You know the kind of thing—classic urban folklore about tourists who wandered away from the bus and got accidentally up-loaded, condemned to Hell for real, and for all eternity. All non-sense, of course—everybody knows that, no matter how things seem when you're in the tank, your mind can't really be decanted from the tender prison of the flesh—but knowing it and feeling it are two dif-ferent things, and we were four days into the tour, so committed to the illusion that we could even talk freely about reality. Anyway, the myths of contemporary oral culture are always there to remind us of the precariousness of our self-knowledge; no matter where you go you can't ever get away from them.

The chasm of serpents was very impressive. I'm not particularly nervous of snakes myself, although I could tell that Matilda was by the way she moved closer and closer to me—and when the slithery things began to move through the flesh of the people they were tor-menting, merging and exchanging flesh, she clung so tightly that she might almost have been trying to do the same thing. To me it was just a promise of mergers of a nicer sort but on her side there was genuine anxiety and authentic horror.

I could feel the release of tension in Matilda's muscles when we moved into the circle where the sinners were shrink-wrapped in their dinky individual flames. That was only a rest-period, of course—a calculated let down before the savage stuff, to which we were deliv-ered once lunch was safely over.

Even as a show, it was hard to take: the mutilations, lacerations and afflictions of horrid disease; the breaking limbs, the tearing flesh and the suppurating wounds. Virgil's commentary, which told us that these were the most heinous sinners of all—the flatterers, forgers and falsifiers—struck just the right note of black comedy, adding to the horror rather than undermining it.

"Well," said Matilda, "there you have it. All the worst sins begin with F—or so they thought in the fourteenth century. Nowadays, of course, we've got as far as G."

"Germ warfare and genocide?" I suggested.

"Government," she said, decisively.

"Oh yes," I said. "Flattery, forgery and falsification all rolled into one. In Dante's day, they hadn't invented democracy—or if they had they had enough sense not to practice it." I was rather proud of that, but her laugh was a trifle tokenistic. I figured that she must be real; Turings always overdo the sense of humor for fear of seeming unemotional.

It was difficult to believe that there could be any more Hell to come after all that, but there was. As afternoon turned to evening we passed the giants and eased out way on to the lake of eternal ice, with all its embedded victims.

By now, all the members of our party seemed to have crystallized out into couples, and that lent an extra poignancy to the fact that so many of the icebound were fixed in pairs, frozen in acts of ruthless violence, with expressions of pure hatred on their frosty faces.

The final image of the three-faced and massively-winged King of Hell, with each of his three mouths chewing away with such evident relish, was the perfect climax to the day on which Matilda and I were set to get together properly. Even in a gel-tank your body builds up muscular tensions that need to be discharged, and the horrors of Inner Hell really did build up to quite a pitch. It was a real relief to be able to discharge all the day's tensions.

Matilda had a good time too—and when morning came there was nothing like the rapid cooling my relationship with Sophia had undergone. I was glad about that, because a second blow to my ego might actually have done some damage, and that might have made our day in Purgatory too purgatorial by half.

* * * * * * *

SOME OF THE others obviously found Purgatory far too tame after the excitements of Malebolge but I really didn't mind. I like to savor my pleasures, and I find that a little peace and quiet helps me to take full advantage of the Morning After feeling. All the dutiful angels with swords of flame were okay by me, and even the people laboring under yokes or the weight of massive stones didn't seem overly tedious. I can appreciate subtlety as well as colour, and Matilda was just as sensitive. It was good to be able to put a protective arm around her when we passed the quiet ranks of those with needles in their eyes.

Even I had to admit, though, that the Gardens of Tantalus weren't much of a spectacle. It's hard for people of our era to identify with starving souls forced to insatiable contemplation of trees laden with luscious fruit. Fruit simply doesn't have the same significance nowadays as it had in the days before factory farms. Nobody picks food any more; whatever grows on trees is purely for ornamentation.

When I made that point to Matilda she was quick to agree. "It's the same with the mountain," she observed. "Nobody climbs mountains any more; they're just something to be looked at and admired. The symbolism's all wrong for the modern era. Not that it's too much, of course...just that it's all screwed up. I don't think there's anything to be done with it. Hell will always work, after a fashion, but Purgatory can't—not any more. It's redundant."

"It's in the book," I reminded her. "Anyway, you can't go straight from Hell to Heaven. You need an in-between."

She smoothed her long black hair with her right hand, then touched her fingers to her throat. "Oh, I don't know," she said. "Are they really as far apart as we pretend?"

I have to admit that the final circle of Purgatory really was a disappointment. It wasn't so much that it was repetitive—oh look, yet more people packaged in flame, ho hum—but that all the singing struck such a bathetic note. Getting to the top of the mountain rounded off the day all right, but I really could have done without the choral accompaniment.

On the bright side, Virgil told us that it was now time for him to bow out, and that Beatrice would be our guide for the remainder of the trip. I think everyone was glad to see the back of the old man; his lecturing style had gradually taken on the tired drone of a lazy bee—forgivable, maybe, in a real person, but never in a Turing.

Maybe I was more than usually inclined to be bored by what was going on outside because I was looking forward to the second night with Matilda. For me, second nights are usually better than first nights—more relaxed, easier all round—and I'd tacitly assumed that it would be the same for her. As the evening progressed, though, she became a little fretful.

I realized that I might have congratulated myself too soon on having avoided another embarrassment of the Sophia variety. I began to think, too, that Matilda wasn't so very different from Sophia. She liked to project an image which implied that she had depth, but in the final analysis she was only doing it in the hope of concealing how shallow she really was.

Matilda and I did spend a second night together, but it was clear to me that it would probably be our last; there was a make-the-most-of-it fervor which was rewarding in its way but a little sad. On the other hand, I'd noticed during dinner that Helen and her well-padded partner seemed to be coming unglued at last, and I'd begun to wonder whether there might be a possibility of engineering a swap.

The Earthly Paradise would have been a nice place to experience another Morning After glow, but in the circumstances the glow in question didn't have quite the right feel. Matilda and I were already drifting apart, no longer bothering to contrive witty exchanges. Beatrice was a clever commentator—I could tell right from the start that I was going to like her a whole lot better than Virgil—but I wasn't in the mood for more singing, and singing was unfortunately what we got.

The sphere of light was like any light-show, and the supposedly-wonderful things which came to gaze through the windows of the observation-deck weren't a patch on the demons of Malebolge. I suppose that's an odd thing to say, given that the demons were designed as archetypes of ugliness while these angelic forms were supposed to embody the epitome of beauty, but it's the way I felt. That kind of abstract and ethereal beauty may be pretty, but it just isn't interesting—not, at any rate, in the context of a virtual holiday. Tourists have always found beauty in landscapes, but the landscapes in question have to be *dramatic*. The sphere of light was too soft and too bright.

It wasn't until we began the journey across the planetary spheres that we got any real sensation of vastness or strangeness, and that was initially spoiled, for me, by the fact that Matilda and I had finally arrived at the parting of our ways. It was, as they say, a perfectly amicable split—but it still left me feeling worse than the split with Sophia.

As things turned out, though, the break-up with Matilda was a beginning as well as an end. I'd been right about Helen, and the all-change was engineered peacefully enough over a very nice lunch. I don't know what tastes the tour company had blended to serve as nectar and ambrosia but it was a real triumph of food science; I've supped a lot of manna in my time but I'd never had it sweetened like that before.

"A light show is just a light show," I said to Helen, generously sharing my enlightenment, "but importing Heaven into a taste is a real touch of genius.

"Are we at Heaven now, then?" she enquired, innocently—giving the impression that she hadn't heard a word Beatrice had said.

"Not quite," I agreed. "Heaven has its borderlands too, just like Hell. We're still ascending through the crystal spheres of the Ptolemaic cosmology."

"It's funny how they used to think the Earth was flat and the sun went round it," she said. "I suppose it was an easy mistake to make though, in the days before round-the-world yacht races."

I've been on tours of the real solar system, of course, and I've done the full interstellar circuit, black holes and all. The closed cosmos of the crystal spheres could easily have seemed tame after that, but once we'd had lunch I was feeling ready for wholehearted recommitment to the illusion and I made a concerted attempt to pull myself together. I was on holiday, after all; I had a duty to enjoy myself as much as I possibly could, even in Heaven.

"Maybe it's paradoxical," I said to Helen, "but there's a sense in which the kind of local, restricted vastness embodied in the Dantean cosmos actually impacts more on the imagination than authentic vastness. Because it's finite, you can get a manageable sense of scale that the infinite simply doesn't give you."

"I know what you mean," she said. That was when I decided that she had to be real too—a Turing would have played dumber.

The Dantean planets were quaint, of course, and distinctly crude by comparison with their actual counterparts, but that was half the fun. As we moved further and further out towards the sphere of the fixed stars I began to appreciate the fact that most of the others—including Matilda and Sophia—had gravitated to the far end of the gondola. The stately ascent was the kind of sensation best savored in relative isolation.

Although I wasn't paying overmuch attention at the time, I'd be prepared to bet that a lot of the pairings that hadn't already split came apart that afternoon. Even at a distance I noticed that Sophia was giving out signals of renewed availability, but I didn't regret not being in a position to respond.

When we floated into the Sun of Angels, Beatrice told us that Dante had been unable to perceive that part of his journey, comparing it to the innocence that attends thoughts arising in the mind. The tour company, being past masters in the light-show business, had no such difficulty—and although they ran into the inevitable problems attendant upon the fact that yet another light-show is yet another light-show, I was both ready and willing to let it all flow over me.

Unfortunately, there are times when being ready and willing aren't quite sufficient.

The glorious spirits of the great theologians were imposing enough, but it was a real mistake to have them singing and dancing. I understand the requirements of fidelity to the original as well as any man, but there was no way the scene could have been made to work. The more voices joined in with the Heavenly Choir the more absurd it became, and the harp-music really didn't help. I dare say that it was all very Doré, but it simply wasn't enough.

"I don't think this is going to work," I murmured to Helen.

"Give it time," she said.

It wasn't until we set foot on the stairway of gold leading up to the Seventh Heaven that I realized why we hadn't been disembarked from the gondola before, even on stopovers. The sudden removal from what had become intimately familiar surroundings did lend some much-needed impact to what would otherwise have been a tired cliché. The splendors swirling around the stairway would have been one more phase in the overextended light-show if they hadn't served the dual function of isolating us from one another, giving the appearance that even though we were elements of a crowd we were each alone with the image and voice of Beatrice—who now floated free in the liquid air instead of looking down at us from the gondola's podium.

Helen held tight to my hand, but that only emphasized the fact that I couldn't see her.

St Peter wasn't any more impressive by virtue of being seen without the intervention of a virtual window, but the trick of making Adam a reflection of every beholder—even the women—was oddly effective. The ranks of angels circling the Divine Light were colorful enough, but Beatrice's explanations had begun to get a little tedious and it was a relief when she drifted away. We all knew by then that there was nothing left to come but the big crunch.

It was party time, and God was to be our host.

* * * * * * *

I SUPPOSE THERE was no way for the tour to end that would have provided a better climax. It isn't so much that we live in a world where no one actually believes in God; lots of people still do, or still pretend to. It's more to do with the kind of belief we have. Even if God hadn't been so comprehensively dethroned by the passage of time—and for some of us, at least, I assume that He hadn't—He'd have been bound to appear very differently to us than he did to Dante. Dazzling light can't possibly suffice as an impression of divinity in a world that has far more light than it can ever need, and nothing that could possibly be inserted into that light—however obliquely—could possibly appear to us as anything other than it really was: a carefully-synthesized image.

Art has lost its innocence since Dante's day; it can't be mistaken any longer for anything but itself. The tour-designers knew that, and they were wise not to enter a competition they couldn't win. They were wise, too, to use the reflection gag as a throwaway; it would have been a real let-down if God, rather than Adam, had been wearing our own face.

The way they rigged it was that he wasn't wearing any particular face at all. His features were fluid, incessantly mobile—all except for the eyes. The eyes were steady and sharp, very bright and very wide. You could almost believe that not a sparrow fell unnoticed or uncared for. The real trick, though, was in the positioning. When the light faded out we didn't see the staircase again, nor one another. I could still feel Helen's hand in mine but in visual terms I was alone at the centre of the universe, looking into infinity—and God was outside, looking in.

They didn't drag the moment out a second longer than was necessary. The light came back, and the crowd with it. From then on, it was paradise as fairground, paradise as bean feast, paradise as song and dance—all at once. It wasn't the end, because we'd already seen the end; it was just a long and hearty goodbye.

It was a good party—not a great one, but a good one. Everyone had a sense of having some catching-up to do, and everyone put their heart into the business of completion in spite of the fact that the surroundings lacked authentic excitement.

I was glad that I'd finished up with Helen, when the time came for the final retirement, not because the sex was better in any mechanical sense but because I felt by then that we were really communicating. We hadn't a lot to say, but we never let go of one another's hand after we'd looked into the staring eyes of God.

Sometimes, the words—and the ideas behind them—can get in the way. Sometimes, a healthy measure of tongue-tied innocence is exactly what you need, and there's no better time than when you're coming home from Heaven.

She was real. I had no doubt about that, but I didn't offer her any information about myself and I didn't ask her for any. It's best to leave holidays self-contained, in my experience. Even if we were to meet in some other virtual reality, it wouldn't have been the same. *We* wouldn't have been the same. Only Turings stay the same while they move from one virtual world to another, and even Turings don't *seem* the same.

We'd been through Heaven together, and I was glad about that, but Helen wouldn't have been Helen anywhere else, and I wouldn't have been me.

* * * * * * *

I SUPPOSE, ON due reflection, that the one trouble with the Divine Comedy Tour is that it tries to do a bit too much, and in a rather inconvenient order. I think the pace is a little too hectic, even at the Heavenly end, when things become so much more relaxed. I can't help wondering whether it's absolutely necessary to stick to the order of the book as well as the substance. Suppose, for instance, you could start with a little taste of Hell, just as a teaser, before getting Purgatory out of the way on day two. Then you could go back for a more leisurely look at the Inferno, maybe alternating the icy parts and the hot bits for the sake of contrast, before taking a quick loop through Paradise—with much less singing and not so much light-show—with a whole day to spare. Then, you see, you could hold the final party in the hottest part of Hell, with demons for company instead of angels and real fire underfoot.

I know that a scheme of that kind would be confused as well as un-Dantean, but it seems to me that, in an odd sort of way, it would be truer to life. All things considered, though, I enjoyed the tour pretty well. I don't think I'd go again, even if they rejigged it along the lines I've suggested, because I've seen it all now and there's not a lot in it that I feel I could get more out of if I saw it twice, but I'd gladly recommend it to anyone in the chat room—and whatever anyone else might say, it really is better to go with a group.

Maybe, in the final analysis, we *are* all alone inside our suits, inside our heads and inside our souls—but whether you're in Heaven or Hell, or just the old daily grind, it's surely easier to face up to the fact if someone else's hand is holding tight to yours.

VICTIMS

It was Stephen Swalecliffe's own idea to call his first exhibition "Victims." I didn't think it was a good idea at the time, but Stephen isn't the kind of artist to listen to his agent's advice. Some still say, even now, that he isn't really an artist at all, but that's utter nonsense. He's *the* artist, not merely of the 2010s but of the entire twenty-first century, and it isn't simply the fact that he's my meal ticket that makes me say so. Even if I weren't his agent I wouldn't be able to think of any other modern artist who has achieved such a remarkable synthesis of the representational and the conceptual. The man is an authentic genius.

"They don't *look* like victims," I told him, when he first showed me around his studio. "It's all very well to give them titles like *Roumanian Orphan* and *Rapee*, but that's not what you've put into their faces. They don't seem anguished. In fact, they all seem quite tranquil—especially *Junkie* and *Redundant Miner*—and the expressions of self-satisfaction on the faces of *Leukaemia Sufferer* and *Ninety-Nine Years Old* surely give the lie to their supposed wretchedness. Okay, so they're all lying down instead of standing erect, but it seems to me that it would be more effective, as well as more accurate, simply to call them sleepers."

"They are victims, Charles," he told me, firmly. "Every last one of them. They don't wear their anguish on the outside, but that's evidence of their courage and hopefulness. They've laid themselves down *because* they're victims, because they've become thoroughly sick and tired of being victims, and because they've decided to take the chance to be something else instead."

I didn't put up too much of a fight. The last thing I wanted was for Stephen to start wondering whether he'd be better off with another agent. I knew that his stuff would sell, and I was pretty sure that, once his prices took off, they'd keep on rising. Sculptors aren't nearly as prolific as painters and there's a great deal more trouble involved in showing their work, but the good ones are worth the extra investment. I'd never expected to encounter one as good as Stephen Swalecliffe.

Before I saw the first thirteen pieces in his Brixton studio I would have said that reclining nudes had been done to death and that supine ones were merely stretching the cliché. I would also have said that flesh-colored statuary was a bad idea, because the results always look like waxworks that couldn't make it to the plinths at Madame Tussaud's. Almost as soon as I stepped through the door of his workroom, though, I revised my opinion. Even at first glance, Stephen's work was the kind that required all received wisdom to be consigned to the dustbin.

"They're made of glass!" I said, as soon as I touched *Battered Wife*. "I thought they were plastic."

"They're vitrified," he agreed. "Actually, glasses and plastics aren't so very different, in terms of the underlying physics. They're all supercooled liquids that set hard without undergoing the kind of abrupt crystallization which causes a fundamental change of state. Window-glass is inorganic, of course, whereas polystyrenes and the like are long-chain carbon molecules, but most organic substances can be vitrified in such a way as to produce a texture much more reminiscent of window-glass than polystyrene. It usually requires very low temperatures, but the work on cryoprotection I did while I was in California threw up some interesting spin-off...."

"So it's *not* glass," I said, trying to keep things simple.

"It all depends what you mean by *glass*, Charles," he replied, a trifle wearily. Scientists hate simplicity, and Stephen Swalecliffe had been a scientist for fifteen years before he accepted that his true vocation was to be an artist. He did try to continue the scientifically pedantic explanation, but I didn't even try to keep track of it or pretend to be listening. I don't think I'd ever heard the word "cryoprotection" before, and I certainly didn't know what it meant.

Everybody teases me now because I never asked what seems to them—in retrospect—to have been a very obvious question, but it's not the sort of question that anyone seriously involved in the art world could have voiced. Reclining nudes and naturalistically colored statues are bearably trite, but the idea of sculptures that aren't really sculptures but corpses dressed up with wax or clay is the worst of all horrid clichés—the stuff of the corniest horror movies. *Of course* I didn't ask Stephen Swalecliffe whether he'd assembled a company of actual victims and persuaded them to allow him to turn them to glass. I never entertained the least suspicion, not even for a moment. You could have knocked me down with a feather when the CID waltzed in on day three of the exhibition at the Hartley Street Gallery and arrested my latest protégé for multiple murder.

* * * * * * *

I WAS DELIGHTED when Arthur Such—a canny old soul from a firm of solicitors recommended by Daddy—came back to me with the good news that Stephen intended to plead *not guilty* to all the charges, and was convinced that he could clear his name.

"I knew it was ridiculous," I said. "The leap of the imagination required to conclude that they're actual bodies rather than accurate images is so absurdly reckless that I can't imagine why the police didn't simply refuse to entertain it. When will he be released?"

"Oh, he admits that they're the bodies of real people, Mr. Carnforth," Such informed me, airily. "He just denies that they're dead. He claims that they're in a state of suspended animation, and that he hasn't done them any injury whatsoever. Quite the reverse, in fact. He says that he's given them all a ticket to an indefinite but possibly better future, and a means of paying their fare."

"Paying their fare?" I echoed, quite dumbfounded.

"In exchange for putting them into a state of suspended animation they gave him the right to exploit their vitrified bodies commercially, for a period of not less than ninety-nine years. The contracts they signed allow him to exhibit them as works of art and to lease them to galleries or private collectors for periods not in excess of ninety-nine years. The contracts are do-it-yourself jobs, which may turn out to be not worth the paper they're typed on, but at least he made the effort."

Prior to that moment I had thought that Stephen's insistence that none of his "sculptures" should be sold until the exhibition had run its course was mere affectation. He hadn't given me the least warning that what I would eventually be negotiating on his behalf would be leases rather than sales.

"What you're telling me," I said, hesitantly, "is that I've been taken for a ride—exploited by a con man."

"Not at all. Dr. Swalecliffe asked me to assure you that he still considers you to be his agent and that he remains confident that you will not find the role unlucrative. He insists that he never actually lied to you—he merely refrained from telling you exactly how he produced his so-called works of art. He says that if you'd only bothered to listen to his discourse on cryoprotection—or even to look the word up in a dictionary—you'd probably have been able to figure it out for yourself. He strongly suggests that you retain the arrangement you made with him, because, if and when the jury at his trial find him not guilty, the precedent will clarify and firmly establish his right to exhibit and lease his works. I've advised him that the matter's not nearly as simple, legally speaking, and that settling the complex issues involved could well tie us up in court for years, but Mr. Swalecliffe doesn't seem to be intimidated by that prospect. He expressed his firm conviction that the publicity generated by his trial will send the price of his works *sky high*. His phrase, of course."

"You're joking," I said.

"I'm merely reporting what Dr. Swalecliffe told me," the solicitor retorted, primly. "He did not give me the impression that he was joking. When I tried to impress upon him the seriousness of his situation, as seen from my point of view, he agreed that it was indeed very serious, and that he intended to treat it as such."

I thought about my own situation for a few moments, recalling the trouble that *avant-garde* artists of the '90s had got into when they'd begun obtaining bits of dead people from mortuaries for use as raw materials. There were, apparently, all kinds of rules and regulations regarding the disposal of corpses, which could be very inconvenient for an agent trying to flog art-works made from dead human flesh. If Stephen Swalecliffe's works weren't actually dead, however, an entirely different set of precedents came into play. No objection had been raised to Tilda Swinton lying in a glass box for days on end in the same hectic decade, because the box wasn't subject to the health and safety regulations normally applicable to places of work.

"If the supposed victims are still alive," I said cautiously, "there won't actually need to be a trial, will there?"

"Interesting point," Such observed. "My client has already been charged with all thirteen murders, even though *Roumanian Orphan* has yet to be properly identified, and the CPS aren't likely to drop the charges unless they can be provided with acceptable proof that the alleged murder-victims are not, in fact, dead. In the light of Dr. Swalecliffe's statement, I have applied for a court order requiring the coroner to desist from attempting to conduct a *post mortem* examination of any of the alleged victims, and I will shortly apply for them to be made wards of court until the matter of their status can be conclusively settled. I may have to resort to *habeas corpus*, but I presume that all the interested parties will eventually be able to agree on the matter of suitable temporary accommodation for the disputed items. At present, however, it doesn't seem likely that we shall be able to agree on a timetable for the provision of proof of innocence."

Solicitors can be almost as difficult as scientists when it comes to speaking in layman's terms, but I could see where he was going.

"You mean that Stephen won't reanimate them to order?"

"Exactly," said the solicitor agreed. "Dr. Swalecliffe has pointed out to me, rather emphatically, that the contracts he made with his clients contain rigidly restrictive specifications as to the conditions in which premature reanimation might be permitted. His view is that he is under an obligation to all his clients to maintain them in suspended animation for the agreed terms, unless and until those conditions are met. As I've already pointed out, the legality of these contracts might be disputable—but Dr. Swalecliffe has persuaded me that my clear duty, at least for the time being, is to protect his obligations as best I can. The burden of proof does, of course, lie with the prosecution."

"So what you're saying," I said, as I struggled to keep up with the state of play, "is that it's up to the opposition to prove that they're dead, rather than Stephen having to prove that they're alive—and because you won't let the coroner cut them up, that's not going to be as easy as they'd like it to be."

"Put crudely," Such agreed, "that's about the size of it."

"So they *will* put him on trial—and it'll be up to a jury to decide how plausible his claim is that they're still alive."

"That seems to be Dr. Swalecliffe's preferred outcome," Such admitted. After a moment's further thought, he added: "I think I can probably obtain it for him."

It was at that point that I began to realize what Stephen Swalecliffe meant by "sky high." He might have been a mere amateur in the publicity and promotion business, but as a scientist he obviously knew that the sky is a hell of a lot higher than any mere art expert had ever been able to suppose.

* * * * * * *

THE NORMAL COURSE of modern trials, as I understand them, is that the prosecution fields a couple of so-called experts who swear on the Bible that one thing is true, and then the defense trots out a couple of their own, who swear that the opposite is true, leaving the jury to pick the most plausible or toss a coin. The prosecution in the case of *Rex versus Stephen Swalecliffe* obviously didn't want to descend to that kind of lottery. They lined up a prodigiously long and very impressive series of eminent scientists to serve as expert witnesses. Every one of them swore on oath that it was impossible for human beings to be successfully revived after being put into suspended animation. There was a lot of technical stuff about the viability of the deep-frozen corpsicles currently being stored by American Cryonics Corporations, and a lot more about the possible relevance of that kind of work to Stephen Swalecliffe's vitrification technology.

I'm no expert, but so far as I could judge, all the world's cryogenicists seemed to be queuing up to explain the logic of using cryprotective agents to prevent cells from being damaged by crystal-formation as body temperature was lowered. The ones who couldn't get on the prosecution's list went on TV instead. All of them were united, however, in condemning Stephen's contention that if you had good enough protection you didn't actually need the very low temperatures. I soon became bored with accounts of Arctic frogs spending months on end in a vitrified state at temperatures of thirty or forty degrees below zero, and all the convoluted arguments supposedly proving that there was no possibility at all that any analogous process could be made to work at temperatures between ten and thirty degrees above zero.

That was the entirety of the prosecution's case. Stephen Swalecliffe's "Victims" couldn't possibly be alive, and because there was no dispute as to who had consigned them to their present state, Stephen Swalecliffe had to be judged guilty of murder. The waiting world could easily see, however, that the case had one fatal weakness. Henry Caldecott QC—the barrister briefed by Arthur Such—didn't need a battery of experts to refute the evidence of the prosecution's experts. All he needed was one single witness drawn from the ranks of the alleged victims.

The contracts that Stephen and his clients had signed were very specific about the lengths of time that each one would remain in suspended animation but there was an escape clause which allowed for temporary revival in circumstances which subjected either party to "severe and mortal danger". Stephen and Arthur Such had flatly refused to allow any of the "victims" to be reanimated before the trial, but they both took the view that once the prosecution had completed its case the necessary conditions would be fulfilled.

The matter seemed simple enough to me, and to the millions following the trial in the newspapers, but lawyers will be lawyers. It took three weeks of esoteric wrangling to determine that Stephen would be allowed to carry out the reanimation procedure himself, in private, in order to protect his intellectual property rights in his as-yet-unpatented process. No other judgment would have been sensible or just, but a court of law is the last place where the obvious can be taken for granted. Fortunately, common sense prevailed in the end, and Stephen was allowed to go to work on the victim of his choice.

I shall never forget the moment when Doreen Grey—formerly known as *Rapee*—went into the witness-box. If the trial had taken place in America there would have been cameras and legions of photographers, but England is the last place on Earth to maintain the commercial privileges of sketch-artists. The scribbling was positively furious—almost as furious, in fact, as Doreen Grey.

Technically, of course, Doreen Grey's mere appearance in the court was sufficient to collapse the prosecution case. The CPS barrister should probably have applied to drop the whole thing before she even reached the court-room, but he didn't. Maybe he was hoping that she'd show evidence of brain-damage or some other unlooked-for side-effect that would have allowed the CPS to go after Stephen for a lesser crime, but I think he knew well enough that he was part of an epoch-making event and didn't want to throw away his chance to conduct a cross-examination that would be historic in spite of its futility.

Stephen Swalecliffe never took the stand himself, reserving his account of his motives, ambitions and prices for fee-paying interviewers. It was left to the eccentrically articulate Doreen Grey to explain both the logic and the aesthetics of her admittedly-risky decision to exchange the nasty, brutish and short span of ignominy currently available to ordinary citizens of the United Kingdom for an extended lifespan as a work of art—plus, of course, the possibility of reawakening in a future where immortality would be routinely available to the citizens of a technological Utopia.

"What do you suppose the wife of Francesco del Giocondo would have said if Leonardo da Vinci had offered her the choice that Stephen Swalecliffe offered to me?" Doreen asked the court, rhetorically. She then switched into a squeaky falsetto that is extremely unlikely to have resembled the way that Leonardo da Vinci spoke. "See here, dearie, you can either carry on getting older till you die, until nothing is left of you but an image that might or might not become world-famous and hang for centuries in the Louvre, or you can *become* that image, with pretty much the same chance of being hailed as a masterpiece and gawped at by generations of tourists, but always hanging on to the option of jacking it in and having another go if ever the world becomes a much less cruel and shitty place than it is today."

Doreen paused for effect, and the crowded courtroom held its collective breath while we waited for the inevitable answer.

"*Sod that old git Francesco and the fucking oil paints*, she would have said," Doreen proposed, with crushing logic. "*I want to be the Mona Lisa*. Well, so did I—and I still bloody well do, so why don't you interfering mother-fuckers just fuck off and let me get on with it?"

I won't say that I couldn't have put it better myself, but it certainly did the trick. It was the greatest coup in art history. Oh what a joy it was, on that glorious day, to be Stephen Swalecliffe's agent!

* * * * * * *

ARTHUR SUCH AND Henry Caldecott QC were more than pleased, because the various corollary civil actions dragged on for years. Some of them are still going, in fact. Stephen's DIY contracts made lucrative work for a dozen lawyers for a decade and more, but the hold-up didn't stop the cash flowing into Stephen's coffers—and, of course, the coffers of Carnforth and Associates.

There's nothing like a little anxious anticipation to boost speculation, and the hypothetical value of the thirteen "Original Victims" kept going up and up. It's remarkably easy to turn hypothetical value into real cash if you understand the theory of banking, and that's one area in which I can really hold my own. The fact that Daddy Carnforth's in the business helps enormously.

Stephen didn't couch his own explanations in the graphic terms favored by Doreen Grey, but he was equally eloquent in his own way. "I realized early in my career as a researcher in cryoprotection," he wrote—for the very modest fee of thirty pounds a word—"that the real problem faced by Cryonics Companies was one of maintenance. It costs money to keep bodies deep-frozen, and while they're stuck in some vault, bathed in liquid nitrogen, they're not really in a position to earn their keep. It seemed to me that developing a technology of room-temperature vitrification would kill two birds with one stone. The cost of storage would no longer be a problem, and the deanimated bodies could actually earn their own keep by serving as statuary. I always knew that the economic details would be complicated and controversial, and I admit that what I call *constructive slavery* might not, at the end of the day, be universally embraced as the ideal basis of negotiation, but I was sure that the principle was sound—and so it has proved. The demand for living statues has taken off in no uncertain terms, and I think it will increase even further once I've figured out a convenient way to vitrify people while they're standing up or otherwise posed—like, for instance, Rodin's *Thinker*."

114

I must confess that, until the Swalecliffe trial, I'd always been a staunch defender of elitism in the arts. I'd never been in the least interested in all those crusades to bring art to the common people, because the common people, although numerous, simply don't have the money to take a serious interest in art. The essence of Stephen's new art, on the other hand, is that it provides scope for people who could never earn a decent living as active individuals to get fully involved in the world of art. Many previous artists had given common people a role in their work by using them as models, but Stephen has gone far beyond that.

Some people thought at first that it was a mere affectation on Stephen's part to refuse all applications for vitrification by the rich and the famous, but his principles were soon recognized as a moral and aesthetic masterstroke. "Let those who can enjoy life be condemned to it!" he said. "Only those who sorely need release should be allowed to become works of art. The essence of my work is the transformation of victims into victors!"

This was stirring stiff, and everyone knew it. If the rich had been allowed to enter suspended animation themselves there would, of course, have been far less money available for the maintenance and aesthetic enjoyment of the statuesque time-travelers, but that was never the point of Stephen's methods of selection. He really is a champion of the downtrodden, a balancer of moral account-books, a redeemer of the unfortunate. To those who challenge his right to "play God" I simply say that "playing God" is what creativity means—and creativity is the very essence of Art.

Stephen's monopoly of his new art form didn't last long, of course, and very few of those who have followed in his footsteps have his high principles. Some people say that he was a fool not to have applied for a patent on his process, but that's nonsense. Once scientists know that a thing can be done, it doesn't take long for them to figure out a dozen subtly different patent-busting ways to work the trick. The real measure of the man is that he found another and better way of keeping the opposition at bay.

If Stephen had introduced his techniques to the world as a mere utilitarian technology his career would have fizzled out as soon as the multinationals muscled in, but because he established it as an art-form, he remains *the* master. The others can vitrify away to their heart's content, but they can't produce authentic Stephen Swalecliffes. At best, their products are copies, at worst, fakes. Nobody wants to be vitrified by anyone else if they can be vitrified by Stephen.

Stephen has always been too polite to comment, but I'm not too proud to point out to anyone who asks that Stephen Swalecliffe is the one and only practitioner of the new art whose technique has actually been proven in that worthiest of arenas, the English High Court. He, and he alone, has demonstrated to the world that his works really are time-travelers embarked on the greatest adventure imaginable. He, and he alone, has shown the world the full measure of the privilege enjoyed by those who obtain ninety-nine-year leases on his works.

There are those who claim that Stephen is taking unnecessary risks by allowing his masterpieces to be displayed in public. The "Victims" are, alas, rather brittle. There is always a risk in transporting them, and those which are exhibited in Tokyo and California are in perpetual danger of being toppled from their plinths and fatally agitated by earthquakes.

Perhaps they would be slightly safer if they were to be locked away in vaults, shrouded in cotton wool—but they are human, after all, and still alive. The thoughts in their heads are stilled and their glassy eyes are sightless, but they belong nevertheless to human society. They should not be locked away like lepers and psychopaths; they should be allowed to live in light, to take the favored positions on the world's stage that were denied them before they underwent their metamorphoses from victims to works of art.

Nor is the benefit of their new role entirely their own, for wherever one of Stephen Swalecliffe's "Victims" stands—or, for the moment, lies—those of us whose heartbeats still take the measure of our lives may see own future selves, our hope not merely of eternity, but of glory.

THE SERPENT

ON THE THURSDAY I drove home from work as usual, leaving the office car park at five past five. I was in a good mood—the phrase "only one more day to go" kept echoing in my head. I was looking forward to the four weeks' leave, thinking of it as an extra holiday. The whole notion of paternity leave seemed so new, so strange, that I couldn't help thinking of it as a stroke of good luck rather than something ordinary, something from which anyone and everyone might benefit. I suppose it *was* a stroke of luck that the firm was so up-to-date, so enthusiastic to capture and keep its young executives that it had put such provisions into its package.

The traffic wasn't too heavy even on that nightmarish stretch of the M25 connecting the M3 to the M4, which had temporarily shrunk to three lanes while they were widening it to seven. I got home about five-forty, put the car in the garage, and breezed into the house as if I hadn't got a care in the world. I called out to Ginny but I didn't think anything of it when she didn't call back or rush to meet me—it was difficult for her to do anything in a hurry, being nine months gone. I must have been pottering around downstairs for ten minutes and more before it finally occurred to me that maybe I ought to take a look.

I can't describe what it was like to open the bedroom door and see all that blood. She'd actually taken the duvet off the bed and put down two bath-towels, obviously expecting that there'd be *some* blood and intending to mop it all up, but she could have had no notion of what would actually happen. Both towels were soaked through and the blood had spread out both sides on to the sheet and through to the mattress. She still had the coat-hanger in her hand, with the hook part straightened out and the rest twisted into some bizarre configuration.

I honestly thought she was dead. I didn't see how anyone could lose that much blood and not be dead, but it seems that these things can be very deceptive. Even though I thought that she was dead, I leapt for the phone beside the bed and punched out 999, hysterically demanding an ambulance. It wasn't until I knew the ambulance was on its way that I tried to take a pulse and realized that she was still breathing. It was then that my fear changed focus, and I felt a cold surge of terror at the thought that the baby must be dead...and it wasn't until the shock of that thought had subsided that I realized that that must have been the whole point—that must have been what she was trying to do.

What other reason could a nine-months-pregnant woman have for sticking a partially unbent wire coat-hanger up herself, except to carry out a ridiculously late abortion?

After that, the fear was displaced by something else. It wasn't exactly horror, more a sharply painful sense of not being able to understand, of there being no conceivable explanation. It made no sense, and there seemed to be no possible sense that it could make. It wasn't just that the word *why?* kept echoing inside my head—the worst thing was the awareness that the question had no imaginable or excusable answer.

* * * * * * *

THE AMBULANCE ARRIVED within five minutes, which was good considering the time of day and the fact that the house is two-and-a-half miles from the hospital. The paramedics didn't waste any time. They hooked up a drip before they even tried to move her—not real blood but synthetic stuff, designed to be reaction-free. They must have pumped three or four pints in before they fetched the stretcher to set beside her. They were very careful—they didn't want the bleeding to start again. Neither of them said a word about the coat-hanger. One of them gently took it out of her hand and laid it aside.

"Will she be all right?" I asked, while they were strapping her on. I was already trying to figure out how they were going to get the stretcher round the bend in the stairs.

"I think so," said the senior paramedic. "It looks worse than it is."

"What about...?"

He didn't let me finish. "Can't tell about the baby," he said. "Touch and go. They're surprisingly tough. Have to see."

They were very clever on the stairs. They took the bend very smoothly, as if they'd had years of practice and as if Ginny weighed nothing at all. We made it to A&E in four minutes flat, without so much as a bump or a sway.

In a way, that was the easy part for me, because I could count it down—every second was a step on the way. Once they wheeled her off into the depths of the department, though, I was stranded in that desolate waiting-area full of drunks and wailing children, not having the slightest idea how long it would be before they'd bring me any news or let me go to see her. I don't mind waiting so much when I know what time I'm aiming for, but sitting there in turmoil, watching the red second hand sweep around and around and around without any sign of progress was hell on earth.

It was eight-fifteen when the doctor finally came out.

"Your wife's stable, Mr. Coxon," she said. "The baby's heart is still beating, and there's no sign of any damage to the fetus itself, but we'll have to make a further investigation to determine how much damage has been done to the birth canal. We'll have to do a Caesarean, but we'll have to be careful in determining the right time. For the moment, it's best to leave things as they are, but we're monitoring the situation carefully."

"Can I see her now?" I asked.

"In a little while," she told me. "She's under sedation. She won't wake up for some hours. You'll be able to sit with her if you wish, but...I'm afraid there are some questions I must ask you first."

It shouldn't have come as a shock. I should have spent the previous two hours rehearsing my answers—but when I'd asked myself the question it had seemed so utterly unanswerable that I simply hadn't gone on to think about what I'd have to say to others in search of an explanation.

"I don't know," I said, before she could even formulate the question. "I don't know why she did it. I can't imagine."

"Had she been depressed?" the doctor asked. She was trying to be gentle, and there was no accusation in her tone, but her big dark eyes seemed to me to be like black searchlights projecting shadows into my head.

"No," I said, too promptly, and quickly changed the plea. "Well, a little...unusually quiet, tired, *drained*—but you'd expect that, wouldn't you? It's a strain, isn't it? She was bound to feel awkward, uncomfortable. She wanted it over, of course she did. She cursed the kid a bit, when she was kicked or got backache...bound to. Nothing *serious*. Of course she moaned...not nearly as much as I'd have moaned if I'd been blown up like that, with all the other petty discomforts, all the tedious waiting. I thought she was just exhausted, weary, washed out. Not clinically depressed. Not *desperate*."

I don't suppose the doctor's eyes were saying anything, really, but to me they seemed to be saying: How would you know? How closely have you been watching her? How much time have you given to discussing her feelings? *Really* discussing them, intimately? Haven't you been consciously drawing away, throwing yourself into your work, glad of the excuse that you had to get things straight before you started your leave? Haven't you been glad these last few weeks that you were bringing work home, getting over-tired, so that you didn't have to have too much to do with a wife who'd grown so big, so awkward, so ungainly, so....

"We were both looking forward to the baby," I said, in a sort of anguished stage-whisper. "We both wanted the baby. We had everything set up, everything ready. Cot, pram, clothes, nappies...everything short of redecorating the spare room with Peter the Rabbit wallpaper. There was nothing wrong. Nothing."

It all rang true, inside. I was morally certain that it had been true...except that it plainly wasn't. All that blood on the bed, and that stupid twisted coat-hanger, were witnesses whose evidence was beyond doubt. Something *had* been wrong. Very wrong. However much Ginny had wanted the baby, she had tried to kill it. But why? And why *now?* Why a mere three days from the big crunch? What could have happened to change her mind so suddenly, so dramatically? What could possibly have built up so fast, gone so far? And why hadn't I known?

"We'll need to know," the doctor said, doubtless doing her utmost to sound uncritical. "We're obliged to inform social services. It's not a police matter, but you must understand that there will have to be some kind of investigation. I have to notify the hospital psychiatrist."

"Yes," I said, "I understand."

But I didn't understand at all. And I hated myself for not having had the least inkling that any such thing might happen, for not seeing whatever signs there had been, and for not having the least idea, now, what might have been going on in poor Ginny's head when she tried to skewer our child with a partially unbent coat-hanger.

* * * * * * *

"I think you ought to persuade her to talk to me," the psychiatrist said, as if it had to be my fault that she wouldn't. "This is a serious matter, not just because of the reports, and the fact that the child will have to be placed on the At Risk Register, but because we have to know what went wrong before we can begin to put things right."

"I'm sorry," I told him. "She won't even talk to me, not that way. She just keeps saying that she's sorry. Maybe when they've done the Caesarean—but they had to put that off yesterday. It's rescheduled for this afternoon."

He was plainly unsatisfied, with me as well as Ginny. I felt that he must be thinking that the real blame lay with me—that my not having known it was going to happen was glaring evidence of my inadequacy as a husband and parent-to-be. I understood only too well how he might feel that way. How could I not have known? How could I be so utterly ignorant now as not even to be able to venture a hypothesis. After all, we'd been married six months, living together for more than a year. How could I not know her, unless there was something deeply wrong with me?

"Can you tell me anything about her relationship with her parents?" the psychiatrist asked.

"Not really," I said, horribly conscious of the inadequacy of such information as I had. "They were killed in a car-crash eight or nine years ago, when she was fifteen. That was in California of course—she came to England afterwards to live with her grandmother. She didn't talk about them much, but she didn't seem oversensitive about it. She never liked watching *LA Law* on TV, but that didn't seem particularly neurotic. She has photographs of her parents, but she doesn't keep them on display anywhere and she doesn't look at them often. She gets on all right with my Mum and Dad though—absolutely fine. Her grandmother's still alive but she's in a home now—she has Alzheimer's. Ginny and I visit her once a month, but it's...well, not easy to hold a conversation. I never knew her when she was okay, but she looked after Ginny well enough when Ginny first came over. The rot didn't set in until Ginny was at university. That's where we first met, though we didn't get together until after we graduated."

I would have gone on, just for the sake of keeping it going, pretending to be doing some good, but I wasn't telling him anything he wanted to know. From his point of view, it was all a big zero. No obvious traumas, no vivid neuroses. Around me, Ginny had always been rigorously normal.

Maybe too rigorously, I now thought. Once something goes badly wrong, even normality becomes suspicious, not so much a way of doing things as a way of hiding things.

"I'm sorry, Mr. Coxon," said the psychiatrist, "but I don't have any more time right now. It really is important that you persuade your wife to talk to me, as soon as possible. Please do everything you can."

I promised I would, and went back to Ginny. She was still under sedation, but she was conscious. She didn't even seem spaced out, just a little dispirited. They'd given her a room to herself but I didn't suppose it was any kind of privilege; I figured they didn't want her polluting the minds of the other mothers-to-be with her bad example. I guess the last thing a ward full of anxious and fearful expectant mothers needs is someone in their midst who's tried to short-circuit the process with a little do-it-yourself surgery.

"I'm supposed to convince you that you have to talk to the psychiatrist," I told her. I'd always been open and honest with her. I'd always assumed that she was equally honest with me, although no one would ever have called her open.

"That wouldn't be a good idea," she said, dully.

"Why?"

No answer.

"Because they'd take the baby away?" I suggested. "Because they'd lock you up and throw away the key? It's not like that. They really do want to help, you know. Give them credit for that. Do you want them to take the baby away? Hell's bells, Ginny, I'm your husband...I do have a certain interest in the kid. Don't you think you should have talked to me before you...don't you think you ought to talk to me now. What did I do that suddenly disqualified me from deserving an explanation?"

"There isn't one," she said.

"Does that mean you couldn't help yourself? It just happened. It wasn't any kind of decision"

"I was mad."

"But now you're sane again."

She just looked up at me, but the look said no. She was still mad—except, of course, that when you really are mad you think you're sane, so if you think you're mad you can't be. Not really. So they say, anyway. I moved from the chair to the bed and a picked up her hand so that I could hold it and stroke the back of it.

"Tell me, Ginny," I said. "Please tell me. I have to know. We're together in this—you, me and the baby. I have to know what we're up against. Sod the psychiatrist and the social services—they don't have to know, but I do. I'll promise not to tell anyone else if you insist, but I have to know because I'm on your side and I have to know what I'm doing."

She looked at me long and hard, knowing that I was right. She didn't ask me to promise, probably because she knew full well that I wouldn't be able to tell the psychiatrist or the social worker, because if I did...well, it was the kind of thing you just didn't tell a psychiatrist or a social worker, because there's madness and there's *madness*, and it's always better to let everybody else think that you're only a little bit crazy instead of a lot.

She winced at some internal pang, maybe the baby inside her moving. I could tell that she was in pain, but she was fighting it, trying not to let it show, trying not to let it get on top of her. Maybe it was the pain, or just the knowledge that the baby was still alive, still active, still in a hurry to be born...or maybe a combination of all these things. Anyhow, something let it begin to come out, and once it started, there was no going back.

* * * * * * *

"DAD WAS QUITE bright before he started doing the drugs," Ginny said. "Not successful, at least not by his lights, but okay. Competent, charming, nice. Not weird. It was easy to see what Mom saw in him. I loved him, a lot. Mum didn't do the drugs at first, but he got her into it. I guess he infected her with his own dissatisfactions, his own aspirations, his fervor for finding something more. That's very American, you know, very Californian. Everybody wants to be something else, something more. Everybody wants a new ticket in the lottery of life—not just a winning ticket but a new ticket that wins in a new and better way. Dad's parents had been born again, and him too, but in California nobody gets born again just once...well, hardly anybody.

"I don't know what you'd call the organization. A cult, I suppose, though it wasn't exactly a cult...not like the Moonies or that weird crowd that worshipped the atom bomb. In some ways it was more like the cryonics societies whose members wanted their heads frozen so that they could be resurrected come the time the requisite technology was invented, or the people who took all kinds of drugs that were supposed to keep them young and help them live forever. I think Dad started out on the so-called smart drugs before he got into the designer stuff, the pathway to transcendence, whatever....

"Anyway, the organization didn't even have a name, as such. It wasn't even incorporated, or registered as a religion for the sake of the tax breaks. The members were above that sort of thing. The only handle it had was what its members were supposed to be developing, which was *somatic potency*.

"I was just a kid at the time, you understand—ten, eleven years old. By the time I turned thirteen I'd given up the classes, stopped taking the drugs. I was a ward of court by then, and I was placed with foster-parents as soon as the legal process reached the end of the line. Mum and Dad had visiting rights but the visits had to be supervised and he wasn't allowed to feed me any lines. He wasn't allowed to talk about the organization, so what I know is a little hazy, and maybe even wackier than it really was. But the idea was, as I understand it, that mankind was supposed to be on the threshold of some kind of new evolutionary leap, something that would remake us all—or the favored few, at least—into a new image closer to God's. The time was both ripe and desperate—like, this leap had to be made soon, before the end of the millennium, if the world were to survive the coming ecocatastrophe. I don't know exactly how it was all backed up—a bit of Bible, a smidgen of the Age of Aquarius, lots of fringe science, all kinds of things—but the people in the organization really had a sense of mission, based partly in panic and discontent about the *status quo* and partly in the conviction that they and they alone had the *real answer*.

"The basic idea of somatic potency was that the empire of the mind is still very limited. We only have conscious control over a fraction of the things going on in our bodies, lots of things inside us function independently of consciousness—but according to the organization, it was possible, with the right kind of training and the right drugs, to cultivate a true empire of the mind. They sucked up things like biofeedback—you know, where you can use an ECG display to learn to control your alpha-rhythms, things like that—but they took the whole set of ideas much further. According to these guys, you could learn to cultivate total somatic awareness—become consciously aware of what was going on in every tissue and every cell of your body, and gradually extend that awareness into full control. According to the organization anyone and everyone, given enough time and enough effort, could learn to control, cultivate, and mobilize his or her own immune system so that any and all bacteria or viruses, any and all injuries and cancers, could be zapped without the aid of medicines. And that was only phase one.

"Somatic potency was supposed to make you immune to all ills—they claimed that the placebo effect was evidence not only of what could be done but of mankind's readiness to do it. If you had somatic potency, cancer couldn't get you and AIDS couldn't get you. The development of new skills, physical and intellectual, was supposed to become much easier. You were supposed to be able too take control of your dreams and use dreaming as a kind of arena where these new skills could be developed and practiced. Dreaming, the prophets of organization claimed, was an incredibly powerful personal resource, which was just lying there, waiting to be developed, cultivated and used, as soon as consciousness could secure a proper grip on it. The promises went even further than that—in a nutshell, somatic potency was supposed to turn men into supermen, not exactly overnight but quite possibly within the space of a single lifetime...a lifetime that would, of course, expand as your somatic potency grew. Anyone was supposed to be able to do it, given the right attitude and the right training. The training didn't come cheap, of course, but hey...if what you're buying is freedom from all ills, all pain and death itself, what price is too high? Anyhow, the organization worked like any pyramid selling operation—once you were in and getting deeper you could finance your own program by trawling for new recruits, spreading the word.

"I was in the organization for a couple of years. I did all kinds of weird exercises, some hypnotherapy. I played tapes to myself while I was asleep, spent time meditating and trying to make contact with each of my internal organs in turn. I was supposed to be a good student, although that may have been just what they told my Dad so he'd keep stumping up for advancement stages. I was supposed to be making strides in somatic awareness and control...and I certainly didn't get ill, although who's to say I would have if I hadn't been doing the classes? Maybe I even believed I was getting the awareness—lots of people could sucker themselves into that, though the control came a lot harder. Maybe I just pretended, for Dad's sake.

"It was feeding kids like me the drugs that got them into trouble...they were under investigation for that. That was the way they got attacked in the courts, by the Feds or whoever. The organization closed ranks, of course, held hard to their constitutional rights, but the one thing the courts could do even in spite of all the opposition was penalize them for feeding drugs to kids. The adults couldn't be shifted, but the kids could—kicking and screaming if necessary.

"I didn't go kicking and screaming. I never really wanted to be part of it in the first place...I was never brainwashed. I was only ever along for the ride, even at eleven. I did the classes, but my heart was never really in it. Hell, it was just like extra school, just something I had to do to toe the line. Maybe I did manage to get in touch with my liver and kidneys, or thought I did, but what the hell? What I really wanted to be in touch with was Nirvana—the band, not the place. I didn't want to be parted from Mom and Dad but Dad was getting so weird and Mom so helpless....

"Well, I sure didn't fight as hard as I could have. Maybe I was a fink. Maybe I let them down...not just the organization but Mom and Dad. They were broken-hearted, but....

"They had the smash that killed them while they were traveling home after a visit. I kept telling myself that the smash had nothing to

125

do with Dad being upset, but they wouldn't have been on the freeway at all if it hadn't been for me. I put them there, and whatever somatic potency they'd been able to build up wasn't enough to get them around it or pull them through. It was all because of me. After they were dead, Gran insisted on taking me, and everyone thought that was for the best. A clean break. A new start. Put it all behind me, put it right out of my mind."

She paused, submerged by the tide of memory. No doubt somatic potency was supposed to improve your memory, too, make sure that you could never forget, never put anything behind you, or right out of your mind.

I let a couple of minutes go by before I tried to tell her, as gently as I could, that I didn't quite see what any of this had to do with what had happened. I was careful not to accuse her of anything or mention the twisted coat-hanger. She winced anyway, but I couldn't tell whether it was because of what I'd said or something that was happening inside her.

I looked at the clock. They'd be coming to do the pre-op very soon, getting her ready for the Caesarean. We had less than an hour before they put her under. The red second hand was sweeping round and round the clock-face, as if it were stirring time itself into a vortex.

"Somatic potency," Ginny went on, doggedly, "was supposed to be hereditary. Even if you couldn't get much benefit out of the training yourself...and let's face it, I don't suppose they managed to produce too many supermen or save too many HIV-positives from full-blown AIDS...even if you didn't seem to be reaping the rewards yourself, it was supposed to be doing wonders for your unborn kids. Did you know that a woman has all her egg-cells ready-made long before she's born? They're not like sperms, which get manufactured day by day. When I was in training, all my egg-cells were sitting there inside me. I was supposed to be paying particular attention to them with my emergent somatic awareness. I was supposed to be exerting every bit of whatever somatic potency I had to make sure that they'd be in tiptop condition...to make sure that whatever happened to me, whether I became a backslider, or an apostate, or a common-or-garden failure, they'd get the benefit."

"Oh shit," I whispered, as enlightenment began to dawn. Her face was tight. I could tell that the baby was restless in her womb, maybe getting into position to be born, not knowing that the usual exit-route was all torn up. I wondered whether I ought to call the doctor.

"It's all nonsense, of course," she went on, in a voice absolutely without colour or luster. All crazy. It's just me. I know that...except that I'm not sure, any more, exactly what *knowing* amounts to, or where it stops. I know perfectly well that people can't take command of their dreams, and I certainly know that a person's dreams can't be taken over by someone else, even when that someone else is inside them, sharing their own personal space, being part of their own compound body. Don't you think I know that? But knowing is just a limited form of somatic awareness, an embryonic phase in the evolution of the true mind...a hesitant step on the pathway that leads to the godman. Not the superman—they didn't use that term, because it had been cheapened by the comic books—but the godman. That's what somatic potency is supposed to lead to, if not this generation, then the next...or maybe the next after that, if we're too stupid or too scared to give evolution the kind of boost it needs. But they were just dreams, weren't they? I shouldn't even have remembered them, let alone...."

She stopped again. This time, I didn't let the silence extend so far. "What kind of dreams?" I whispered.

She tensed up, and if I hadn't been holding her hand she'd probably have clutched it to her distended body, but she was still struggling with all her might for control...for whatever somatic potency she had.

"The serpent," she said, faintly. "I dreamed...about the serpent."

I knew that if she'd meant *snake* she'd have said *snake*. Her saying *serpent* called up two things to my mind: the serpent in Eden, which had tempted Eve and caused the Fall, or the line in Lear that says how sharper than a serpent's tooth it is to have a thankless child. I didn't know which one she meant. It could have been either. Except that Ginny wasn't a demon in disguise, and she surely hadn't been a thankless child. I knew that she hadn't.

"What...?" I began, but I didn't have a chance to finish.

"It knows, you see," she said—and now she did seem spaced out, as if she were losing it. "It didn't, at first. At first, it was only *practicing*...practicing being human. That's what cats do, you know. In their dreams, they practice their instincts. Someone cut something out of a cat's brains and the operation made it act out its dreams, and he watched it stalking and hunting and doing all the other things cats have to know how to do in order to be successful cats....

"At first, it just practiced...but it had access to all my memories, all my abilities. It had somatic awareness, self-awareness, awareness of me. It got access to all my secrets, learned everything. It was bright, you know...so bright that it was far too clever for its own

127

good. It knew what I'd done, and what I was. It didn't hate me...oh no, it was above such things as hatred. It didn't even despise me, not really. Even if it had been able to talk to me—which it couldn't, not quite—it wouldn't have accused me of anything right out. It wouldn't have told me that I was an unfit daughter and an unfit mother. It would have been kind, even while it didn't understand. But it knew me better than I knew myself. It had the awareness I'd never quite managed to cultivate, and I knew that it was only a matter of time before it got the control, before it took me over completely and turned me into a zombie. The empire of the mind is like any other empire, you see. It can be conquered.

"It pitied me, I think. It pitied me because I'd gone so far and then stopped, without even knowing how far I'd gone, how close I'd got. It was better than me, you see. It knew better than I ever did how close to the brink I'd been, and how blind I'd been to let them take me away, to make me stop. It knew far better than I did what a fool I'd been, what a useless, thankless thing I was. It knew I'd broken my own mother's heart. It knew I'd killed my father as surely as if I'd put a knife into his heart. It had the awareness, you see, even though it was still waiting to be born. It was beginning...only beginning, but...aiming for control. Control of itself, and control of me.

"I tried to fight it...I really did. I told myself that I was crazy. I was crazy, wasn't I? I mean, none of this was real, or true. All of it was just dreams and delusions. They shouldn't have fed me those drugs, you know. Drugs can have long-term effects...they can affect your egg-cells, your babies still unborn. They said that in court. They put expert witnesses on the stand to say that. Expert witnesses, not crazy people, not cult members, not delinquent parents: *experts*. I knew I was crazy, and that I just had to hang on, hang on until the end. God, how I counted the days, the hours...but all that was helping it, you see...helping it to pity me, leaving the way open for it to ransack my memories and plunder my abilities and use my dreams, *use* my dreams to practice, to learn control....

"I tried to use my own somatic potency against it, just to hold it in check until I could get it out. I fought it so hard, for so long, and I really thought I was going to make it. Just three more days....

"But I wasn't good enough. I was never good enough. Even though it hadn't been born yet, it had more potency than me. The only advantage I had left was brute strength. I just couldn't hang on any longer. Time had run out. I couldn't get through the last few days to the birth. I had to stop it, Jim. I had to stop it turning me into a zombie, a slave, a helpless instrument of some little godling.

"I had to do it.

"Christ, Jim, you have no idea...no idea at all...."

There could be no doubt now that she was in severe pain. Her face was chalk-white and in spite of al her efforts she could hardly talk. The muscles of her face were being drawn into a *rictus* of agony and no matter how hard she fought to stay calm, to keep talking, to keep control, she simply couldn't do it.

"Nurse!" I yelled. "Nurse, for God's sake get in here!"

* * * * * * *

THE NURSE TOOK thirteen seconds to arrive, the doctor another twenty-two. They couldn't have moved any faster. Everything they did they did with practiced efficiency. They were good at their jobs: good and skilful and calm and utterly sure of themselves. I was stranded, left helpless. I didn't know what to do. I didn't know what I was supposed to do or what I could do, but they tolerated that. They didn't send me away, they just worked around me.

All I did was hold Ginny's hand, and I kept holding it all the time...every minute of it. I didn't know what was happening, and I didn't even try to understand. I just held her hand and I did whatever the doctor or any of the nurses told me to do. I only let go to let them scrub my hand with something cold, before they gave me the mask and the gown.

I was there all the way through, watching. I counted the seconds and I counted the minutes, waiting for the climax to come...waiting, as it turned out, for the end.

The doctor was not at fault in any way. I told her that, even though I couldn't tell her the rest. The last time she'd examined Ginny and checked the situation the baby had been perfectly okay, and in the right position. That had only been a matter of minutes before I'd come in to talk to her. The baby hadn't tried to be born—its head hadn't even engaged, or whatever they call it when the fetus gets into position for the long journey down the narrow corridor. There was no way of knowing, no way of anticipating, no way of explaining how the umbilical cord got tangled around the baby's neck—around *her* neck, as it turned out; she was a girl.

A Caesarean section is supposed to avoid the possibility of things like that happening. A Caesarean section is supposed to whip the fetus out without it having to struggle or take risks or get things wrong. A Caesarean section is supposed to put the doctor in control.

But sometimes, even if the doctor does everything right, things go wrong. It's a difficult business, being born. Some babies don't make it, coat-hangers or no coat-hangers.

It was an accident, of course. It would be crazy to think otherwise. Anyhow, even if there were such a thing as somatic potency, which there isn't, it was the baby who was supposed to have it, not Ginny. She couldn't have strangled the baby, even if she'd tried. The baby wouldn't have let her do it.

It was definitely an accident.

The umbilical cord is a strange thing, when you think about it. Is it part of the mother or part of the baby? If an expectant mother had *somatic awareness* where would it end, where would it interface with the child in her womb? And if—you'd have to be crazy even to think about it, but *if*—the child had somatic awareness too, even in advance of being born, where would *that* somatic awareness end and interface?

There's no point even in wondering. That way lies madness, and we have to live in the real world. That stuff about evolving superhumanity was all just craziness or science fiction, best forgotten, best put right out of mind. You have to live a normal life. Dreams are just dreams and serpents can symbolize anything you want them to...anything at all.

Never tell a psychiatrist about your dreams and if you do, never mention the serpent. That's my advice. They can come and take you away, you know. It's not just a scare story. They really can come to take you away. It's best to act normal.

Our daughter's death was an accident. There's not an atom of doubt about that. Ginny was just talking to me, explaining how she'd got into such a sate. She wasn't fighting against the baby. What happened was nobody's fault.

I never had to tell the psychiatrist anything. Nor did Ginny. When the baby was born dead, the whole business of official inquiries and At Risk Registers just collapsed and came apart. When there wasn't a child to be protected any more, all its would-be protectors lost interest and moved off. Ginny came home, and got better. Life went on, as normal. It was our secret, and nobody else's.

It still is.

We'll be much more careful next time—much more. You have to be, don't you? I mean, there are so many ways that parents can screw up their children, even without meaning to.

Too many, perhaps.

One day, it'll be different. One day, we'll have it all under control. In the meantime, we'll just have to do the best we can.

TREAD SOFTLY

IT WAS PEMBERLY who told me about the shop just off the Barking Road where magic carpets could be bought. He should not have done so, according to his own principles. He was not only breaking a confidence but setting a lure before me that could only lead me into trouble—but it was the greatest stroke of luck I ever had.

I met Pemberly in the convalescent hospital at Kimmeridge in August 1917. He had been shipped home from Durban, having stepped on a mine while serving in the King's African Rifles. Surgeons there had amputated his left leg above the knee, and the cauterized stump had become infected. The infection brought back a feverish madness that had first possessed him in Tanganyika. My younger brother had lost a leg at Ypres, and had not survived his own battle with decay, even with the assistance of a barrage of sulfa and a battalion of friendly maggots, so we had something in common even before we discovered our shared interest in the Mysteries of the East. I had been wounded myself, of course, else I should not have been in England either, but the burns had only cost me the use of my right eye and the ability to smile.

I have no idea how Pemberly had fetched up in the K.A.R., having spent fifteen years before the war working for the government in Rajputana, but he must have been far from the ideal civil servant and I dare say that his superiors had been only too glad to let him go, especially to another continent. His father was a baronet and his maternal uncle an earl, but as the youngest of four sons he had been surplus to requirements at home, and must have stepped into the role of black sheep with a certain stylish wantonness. He was inclined to look down on a mere vicar's son—who was not even an officer, having been pressed into the R.A.M.C. as a conscientious objector—but he was grateful for the care that brought him gradually back to sanity. It was the strength of his constitution as much as treatment and care that enabled him to fight off the blood-poisoning, but I played my own part.

131

It was while he was delirious and raving that Pemberly mentioned the dream-weavers of Kharshahar, and there was not another man in the entire Medical Corps to whom the words would have had meaning—but my great-grandfather had been a Company man until the '57 mutiny put paid to all that, and his diaries had been passed down to me with his paltry heirlooms. I, unlike my direly pious father, had not merely read them but had taken them seriously, so I knew of the existence of the Secret Trade, although I had always assumed that it had not survived into the era of Dalhousie's railways.

Such investigations as I had been able to make at a distance of six thousand miles had suggested that Kharshahar, a settlement precariously situated in the north-eastern hills of the Thar Desert, had been obliterated by one of the calamitous monsoon failures that led to the founding of Blanford's Meteorological Department. I had assumed that the art of dream-weaving had died with its famine-stricken population. When I related the history of my own researches to Pemberly, however, he felt obliged to demonstrate the superiority of his own knowledge.

"At least two families of dream-weavers survived," he told me. "Had to go a long way in search of succor, mind. Fetched up among Mohammedans in the Sulaimans. Found it much harder to sell their wares once they were settled. Nothing in the world can persuade a follower of the Prophet that there's any kind of Hindu magic but black.

"I arranged the export of half a hundred carpets myself, but it was a dicey business even before the formation of the Muslim League—impossible now, I should think, even if the craftsmen still have the art. Old Ruscoe complained that more than thirty of them were feeble, and half a dozen spoiled, but I reckon he and Radland were glad to have them anyway. Sold them all, I dare say—except perhaps the ones that were spoiled. Might have one or two of those still tucked away."

How could I not plead with him to give me the address of his London agents? "You'll get nowhere unless you mention my name, mind," he informed me, loftily, "and maybe not then—but if old Ruscoe is still alive, he'll surely remember me."

* * * * * * *

WHEN I WENT up to London on my next leave I found the address that Pemberly had given me easily enough, no more than half a mile from the East India Docks. It was more warehouse than showroom, and its gloomy interior was manned by an equally gloomy caretaker, who could not have been a day under seventy-five. He was alone; the shop did not seem to be doing enough business to warrant keeping the place clean and decently lit, let alone properly staffed—but that was only to be expected. War stimulates demand for many things, but exotic rugs are not among them.

"Mr. Ruscoe?" I asked.

"Radland," he replied, curtly—slightly intimidated, as many people are, by the sight of my face. "My former partner died two years ago."

He knew Pemberly's name, though. "Is that old rascal back in England?" he asked, as if he found the notion astonishing.

When I explained that Pemberly had left his left leg in Africa, but that the rest of him was safe in Dorset, the old man's response was a sardonic smile.

"Well," said Radland, "I suppose he still has his stamping foot—though it won't be much use to him without a fulcrum. If he sent you here in search of money or opium, I've none to offer him. The firm is one step short of ruination and the navy's taken over the other business."

"It's not for him that I'm here," I explained. "He said that you might have a magic carpet in stock."

"Then you're a fool who's been had for a mug," was the prompt retort. "The Turks will lose Baghdad to Allenby before the year is out—best wait until the boys bring their trophies home. Plenty of flying carpets among them, I dare say, if you can only find the formula that will make them take off."

"I'm not talking about fantasies from the Arabian Nights," I told him. "I'm talking about the produce of the dream-weavers of Kharshahar. My name is Arthur Wouldham—as was my great-grand-father's. He was a Company man before the mutiny. If you cast your mind back, you might remember rumor of his name."

Had I not had that second name to conjure with, the old man would never have admitted that he knew what I was talking about—but he *had* heard of Arthur Wouldham, and seemed to think more kindly of that name than he thought of Pemberly.

"Those were the days, according to my father," he said, meditatively. "Kharshahar carpets had quality then—but the art went bad after the second great drought of the '60s. The stuff Pemberly sent us was rubbish. Too much hunger, too little hope. Worthless as luxury items, not much good even as collector's pieces. My grandfather sold dream-weaves to the likes of Byron and Wellington, and my father sold them to Carlyle and Davy—but nothing we had after the

Mutiny could have helped men of that caliber. Oscar Wilde asked for one back in '91, and Yeats after him, but I'd have been ashamed to sell them Pemberly's merchandise."

"So you still have some of them in stock?" I asked.

"We shipped most of them to America," Radland informed me. "No more than half a dozen stayed in England. Ruscoe got what he could for them, but there were some we should have burned. Only one buyer demanded his money back, though. Ruscoe gave it to him, I believe. Reputation of the firm to uphold."

"And Ruscoe took the carpet back?" I said.

It is conceivable, I suppose, that Radland had never bothered to ask that question, of Ruscoe or himself, before I raised it. In retrospect, it seems unlikely, but at the time I was fixated on the possibility of acquiring a magic carpet. It required ten minutes to make Radland admit that Ruscoe was not the kind of man to hand a customer's money back without reclaiming the goods, and a further twenty passed before he condescended to work out where it might have been stored—but that interval seemed small by comparison with the time it took to root around the basement storage-racks until the rug materialized out of the shadows, rolled and wrapped in oilcloth.

Radland needed little encouragement to spread the thing out—he was understandably curious to see the design—but making the purchase was another matter entirely.

I'd never seen a dream-weave before, but I'd read my ancient namesake's account of them. I knew that the only colors the dreamweavers used were red and black, symbolizing blood and darkness, and that the pattern would be an amazingly intricate maze, but I was unprepared for the shape of the carpet, having expected an ordinary rectangle, and for the fact that the lines making up the maze were hectically curved rather than straight.

"I told you it was spoiled," Radland said. "I never saw a perfect square or circle, of course, but this...I do believe it's worse now than when Ruscoe first sold it. It's not supposed to be sensitive when rolled, or capable of growth in the absence of light, but London's a city of six million souls, and spoiled rugs acquire a certain saprophytic quality—metamorphic self-cannibalism. Ruscoe should have burned it. I should burn it."

"I want it," I said.

"Then you're worse than the idiot who believes that carpets can fly," he told me, "and I'd be worse than Judas if I took your money." I could tell that he intended to try anyway. I knew that there was no use in bargaining. When I had persuaded him to name a price, I would not have been able to pay it.

"In that case," I said, "I'll steal it."

I didn't hit him. I'm not a violent man. I could hardly be a conscientious objector if I were. Even when he came at me with the carpet-knife, I didn't intend to hurt him. It was his own excitement that killed him, and his own carelessness in tripping over the edge of the carpet. It wasn't my fault. But I had to have the carpet, and he could not have named a price that I could afford to pay.

* * * * * * *

THERE ARE TURTLES that live for hundreds of years, and trees that live for thousands, but there are microscopic parasites that are effectively immortal, provided that they never meet with a fatal accident. They even multiply themselves, by dividing in two, so that even if thousands meet death by fire, drought, or poison, there are thousands more that live on and on. There are creatures in the microcosm which have lived for millions or billions of years, comfortably housed within the huge assemblies of plant or animal flesh that are their manifold Utopias, their multitudinous self-renewing cataracts of milk and honey.

My great-grandfather knew nothing of such things, so his account of the carpets of Kharshahar was steeped in superstition, but I am the child of enlightened times. I see everything more clearly than he did.

Agriculture and animal husbandry have been blessings to mankind—but imagine what boons they were to those populations of tiny immortals whose paradise was composed of the husk of the wheat, or the wool of the sheep! There are many, I do not doubt, that are consigned to oblivion by industrial processes—but within the clothes that we put on every morning, and the plush of our settees, and the litter on our stable floors, there are invisible empires.

For the most part, those empires ignore ours just as ours ignore them—but not invariably.

There was a time when all human craftsmen and artisans were magicians, although the steam-engine, the lathe and the dye-factory have put an end to it. All manufacture is mechanical and sterile now, save for the fabrications of a few fugitive communities remote from the deadening hand of civilization. Even there it is dying, because every enclave of human society is part of something infinitely vaster, and the whole oppresses all its parts. The old magic is all but gone. This war will surely put an end to it—but its memory is not yet vanished. Nor are the last of its products.

135

I know, although my namesake could not, that although the carpets of Kharshahar are not alive in any gross sense, they are host to immortal and invisible empires. The nature and organization of those empires, devastated fractions of which are all that can be glimpsed on microscope slides, is beyond our understanding, but it is conceivable that they too harbor their artisan-magicians, who once used the dream-weavers for their own arcane purposes even as the dream-weavers used them. For whatever reason, though, the carpets of Kharshahar are responsive to dreams, and the dreams of those who walk upon them are sensitized in their turn. It is a trade, of sorts: the secret trade supporting the Secret Trade.

A Kharshahar carpet is sensitive to daydreams as well as those that visit humans by night, but there is no way to know which are held more precious by the dwellers in the weave. In the same way, the emanations of the carpet affect the reveries of the day as well as the visitations of the night. A man who owns a Kharshahar carpet will not only find his sleep enriched but his consciousness too. The dream-weavers of Kharshahar are merchants of hope, ambition and creativity as well as vendors of hallucination.

But I should not be writing in the present sense. The dream-weavers are extinct and the virtue in a Kharshahar carpet is not eternal. That virtue may survive one owner—perhaps "collaborator" would be a better word—and perhaps two or three, but it cannot last forever. This is not because the invisible empire within the weave is ever annihilated, but rather because its constitution changes. Perhaps its need for human dreams is essentially temporary—an appetite to be sated or a resource to be surpassed—and perhaps there is some other cause, but the consequence is clear. In time, even the finest dream-weave becomes enfeebled, and a Kharshahar carpet becomes a carpet like any other. All my revelations regarding the wonder of such possessions ought, therefore, to be written in the past tense.

The carpets of Kharshahar *were* capable of absorbing and influencing the dreams and daydreams of their owners. They *were* capable of enhancing hope, ambition and creativity—but even the best of them is inert now. Even the one that I owned must surely be inert now.

* * * * * * *

I NEVER TOLD Pemberly that I had the magic carpet. So far as I know, he never heard of old Radland's death, and it was probably not considered suspicious in any case, but I did not want him putting two and two together.

I am not a fool, and I knew exactly what Pemberly and Radland meant when they said that a carpet was "spoiled". They meant that it was more likely to enhance despair than hope, sloth than ambition, destructiveness than creativity. They meant that it was a source of nightmares, offering more glimpses of hell than anticipations of heaven. I understood why the man who had bought the carpet from Ruscoe in the 1890s had demanded the return of his money. I understood why its shifting colors, whose mazy pattern reflected its transactions with the mind of its possessor, had been twirled and twisted into a puzzle that the human eye could barely follow, let alone aspire to solve.

I understood all of that, but I wanted the carpet anyway. Nor did I want it for anyone's use but my own. Kharshahar carpets are useless as weapons because anyone unwary enough to accept a spoiled specimen as a gift would simply conceive a strong distaste for its appearance, roll it up and throw it away. A man who has such a carpet, whatever its proclivities, can only obtain the full benefit of its potency by establishing a careful and conscious relationship with its invisible inhabitants; the magic is a matter of exchange and sympathy, of a mystical union of interest and involvement.

I wanted the magic carpet for myself, because I believed—or, at least, hoped—that I could redeem it. There was a sense in which I had desired a spoiled specimen even more fervently that I could ever have coveted a perfect one, because it offered more of a challenge, more of an opportunity. I had deduced from my great-grandfather's records that all such artifacts begin as reflections of their makers, but that, once they are sold, their owners' become their masters. If the maker and eventual master are in spiritual harmony, the transition is easy; if not, hard—but I firmly believed that, no matter how disadvantageous a carpet's relationship with its maker might have been, a good owner ought to be able, eventually, to superimpose his own personality upon the invisible host within the weave.

I knew that the carpet I obtained from Radland would be a difficult beast to tame, but I believed that I could do it, because of the quality of man that I am.

I do not mean by this that I am an unusually virtuous man, rather that I am an unusually sane one. I am the son of a clergyman, but, unlike my brother, I had the strength of character, even as an adolescent, to become a freethinker. I was then in the midst of the greatest and worst war that has ever afflicted the world, but, unlike my brother, I had the strength of character to remain a man of peace. Lest anyone think that "conscientious objector" is synonymous with "coward", I ought to record that I was at the front for six months, which included the first battle of the Somme. The burns that spoiled my face and half-blinded me are ample evidence of the fact that stretcher-bearers are in no less danger from shellfire than those who carry rifles with bayonets fixed. I have always prided myself on being a man who sees things clearly, even in my dreams; the loss of half my eyesight may have rendered my perception two-dimensional, but had not clouded it at all. Other men have seen me differently, since my injury if not my schooldays, but they have never broken my conviction, or my faith in myself.

That was why I had to have the magic carpet, as soon as I knew that it existed—but I knew that I would have to be patient, if I were to lavish the care and attention upon it that it needed or deserved. I had to put it away until the war was over.

* * * * * *

THE HOSPITAL WHERE I spent the latter half of 1917 and the early months of 1918 was a fair way inland from Kimmeridge Bay, but it was sited on a hill to the east of the village, and the sea was visible through Gaulter Gap from the attics where the orderlies were lodged. The view was delightful when the sun shone, sublime when storms hurried up the channel—but for the last year that I spent there, I was incapable of feeling anything but a desire to be gone. The sea became the stream in which Tantalus stood, its horizon a mocking invitation. When the armistice was signed at last, the more intimate contest began in earnest.

My father's vicarage in Stukeley had been closed to me before the war, but I would not have gone back there even if I had been welcome. In 1914 I had been living in Clevedon, near Bristol, tending the machines for a printer named Priestland and lodging over the shop. I did not expect to find the position still in existence, let alone that he would have held it for me, but I found the old man eager to readapt his business to the opportunities and demands of peace-time, and moved almost to tears by the sight of me. I only had to help him clear four years' worth of accumulated junk from my old room to reclaim it. Mr. Priestland even apologized for the fact that the carpet had been ruined and the bed broken, and would certainly have offered to find me replacements had I not assured him that there was no need. I settled in with alacrity. The situation seemed ideal; my daily labor was sometimes hard but not intellectually demanding, and left my soul free for higher and more difficult work.

I had not noticed any change in my dreaming while the carpet was rolled in its oilskin in a store-room at Kimmeridge. I had had

138

nightmares, but they were no different in kind or intensity from those I had had ever since the first day on the Somme. My day-dreams were entirely taken over by expectations of my use of the carpet, but that required no supernatural influence.

At first, when I spread the carpet over the floor of the room above the print-shop, I was so exhilarated by the enjoyment of my possession that I could hardly sleep at all. Had it been summer I might have slept naked on the carpet without so much as a sheet to compromise my interaction with it, but it was the dead of winter and I had no alternative but to wear a thick nightshirt and seal myself in a sleeping-bag. It was not until the third night that I contrived to fall deeply asleep, and to immerse myself in a dream, which owed nothing at all to my memories of the Somme.

I dreamed that I was a bloodstained corpse wrapped up in the carpet, whose fibers were drinking from my veins, having already imbibed the fluid that flowed from numerous knife-wounds about my torso and abdomen. Dreams will not recognize paradoxicality, so I felt nothing odd in being conscious of being dead. I was interested to observe from within the decay and dissolution of my tissues. The experience was not terrifying; indeed, it was quite calm and strangely reassuring.

"What hope can a man have," my father had once shouted at me, "if he has none of Heaven?" Even in 1910 he thought the world a vale of tears without relent.

"The hope of enlightened life," I had replied then—but the carpet taught me that even the oblivion of death is not something to be feared. It is something that lies beyond fear, in being outside time. I have not forgotten that lesson.

Perhaps the carpet had been used at one time—presumably in India—to hide and transport a murdered man. If so, it had also been used to hide a living child, for I dreamed a few nights afterwards that I was wrapped around by the carpet yet again, taxed this time by tears instead of blood. There was fear a-plenty in this vision, but none of it was mine. It reminded me somewhat of the fears of my own childhood, but I was sufficiently detached from it not to enter into the experience or be subdued by its pressure. Its principal effect was to remind me how far I had left childhood behind.

My dreams became less claustrophobic thereafter, and their impressions vaguer. At times I dreamed that I was exceedingly hot, at others exceedingly cold; sometimes I felt myself so heavy as to be made of lead, sometimes so light as to be hurled giddily about by the lightest wind. I was threatened on numerous occasions by monsters lurking in the shadows, all the more horrible while they could not be clearly seen. Once I felt that all my teeth were becoming loose, crumbling and falling out. More than once I looked into a mirror and saw that my entire face was now burned, and felt the sight of my remaining eye blur and fade as its humors congealed. Once I was in a graveyard when all the graves began to open and a uniformed army of the dead struggled upwards through the fertile mud.

I could understand how innocent dreamers might have found these experiences profoundly disturbing, but I was ready for them, and prepared to meet them with a level head. They were not pleasant, but they did not disturb me. They did not make me doubt my purpose. I was glad to move through them, because I knew that in so doing I was moving towards a worthwhile conclusion, and that I was helping the carpet to cleanse itself of all infection.

Things did not go quite as well by day. Mr. Priestland's two presses had been old in 1914, and they had been busy all through the war with official forms and notices. They were coming to the end of their useful life, and were suffering the consequences. Whenever one or the other broke down I contrived to repair it, but time is money to a printer and Mr. Priestland could not help becoming vexed. Typesetting was his responsibility, not mine, so the mistakes made because his hands were not as agile as they had formerly been could not possibly be laid at my door—but the fact that they were made, and work returned to be re-done, did not improve his temper at all.

"Sometimes," he told me, at the end of January, "I feel as if the war had never ended. Nothing has gone rightly since."

"You would not say that if you had been at Kimmeridge," I told him, "or anywhere else that the war's human wreckage fetched up. The world is spoiled, but it is not irredeemable. It requires time, and good will, but everything will be well again."

"You're twenty-five years old, Arthur," he told me, bitterly. "You'll not say that when you're fifty-five."

In March Mr. Priestland had to hire a boy named Tom Hurley to set the type, because his hands would not be still, but he would not replace either of the presses.

"They'll see me through to the end," he said—and so it proved, but only because the end came much more swiftly than he had anticipated.

* * * * * * *

ON THE FOURTH of April 1919 Mr. Priestland suffered a fit in the shop and had to be taken up to my room while he waited for the doctor. It was the first time he had been in there since we had cleared out all the clutter, and the first time he had seen the carpet unrolled.

"My God, Arthur!" he said, when Tom and I let him down on to the chair. "How can you live with that appalling rug? That pattern is enough to drive a man mad!"

I was surprised, for I had not merely grown accustomed to the mazy swirl but had come to feel entirely comfortable in its contemplation.

"It's beautiful," I told him. "And very, very rare."

By the time the doctor arrived he was dead. The room was full of the stink of his shit—but when the body had been taken away, and the window thrown wide open, the air was purged with remarkable rapidity.

I was anxious lest I lose my lodgings, although Tom and I kept the machines going and the work moving out—but Mr. Priestland's solicitor praised my efforts, appointed me "Manager" and told me to keep the business going as well as I possibly could, until he could find a buyer. I cannot say that it thrived under my authority, but I managed to maintain a sufficient flow of income to pay the suppliers and the boy's weekly wage—and I did not despair.

The carpet had been spoiled, according to Pemberly and Radland, but I did not become melancholy, or slothful, and I certainly did not become destructive. I did my daily work, and I did my nightly work, with all the precision I could muster.

Nor was Mr. Priestland's opinion of the carpet unchallenged, for Tom had been far more impressed with its intricacy. He began to make excuses to come up to my room in order to look at it, and set out more than once to try to trace a route through the maze with the steel-capped toe of his boot, although he always lost the track within a couple of minutes. When he asked me where it came from I told him that it was from an empire far away. He guessed that I meant India, and I was content to confirm the guess.

When Tom died of the influenza in May I could not suppress a pang of relief, because the weekly extraction of his wages had left the takings too short. I had to do the typesetting myself now, but I set about it with a will and found it not too hard, even for a man with one good eye. By the time one of the presses broke down irreparably I only had work enough to keep one going anyway, so it was by no means a disaster.

My mother died in June, also of the influenza, and I had to leave the carpet behind while I returned to Stukeley for a few days. My father's hostile attitude neither astonished nor hurt me. "Still doing the devil's work?" was his derisive greeting, but I did not take the trouble to discover whether he was making a play on words, having misunderstood the significance of a "printer's devil", or whether he was laboring under the misconception that I had been apprenticed to a pornographer.

When I returned to Clevedon, my dreams were haunted more by grief than any apparatus designed to produce terror, but that was only natural. It is a well-known fact that grief sometimes takes odd forms, so I was not surprised that my mother did not figure in them at all. Nor, for that matter, did my former employer or my little colleague. The imagery of the dreams was far more amorphous, featuring bleak and desolate landscapes and black abyssal depths, windswept ruins and baleful swollen moons. I rarely experienced any physical presence of my own in these dreams, but was present in the way that a discreet narrator is present in a story: invisible and intangible and yet all-wise. Sometimes, I felt that I was the mind of the world—not the world in which I actually lived but some other, which had already ended in any meaningful sense, all life having been annihilated upon its surface, abandoning its creator to the burden of an infinite loneliness.

By day, I was far more cheerful. I threw myself into my work even more fervently than before, taking pride in every line and every sheet. Although the print-shop had been twice as noisy when both presses were still active, it now seemed constantly abuzz with a musical clatter, whose cacophonous surface hid plangent cadences and apiary melodies. I always wanted to sing as I worked, and often did, although every time I caught myself doing it and stopped, I could not remember a single syllable that my throat and lips had formed.

Life was not easy, but I was content. And now that the spring was turning into summer I could discard my sleeping-bag and night-shirt at last, and stretch myself out naked on the carpet's cunning maze. The caress of its fibers on my own coarse hide was as tender as it was luxurious, as sensuous as it was welcoming.

* * * * * * *

IT WAS ON the thirteenth of July that Mr. Priestland's solicitor concluded the liquidation of Mr. Priestland's estate by finding a buyer for the print-shop. Unfortunately, the buyer—a Mr. Horrocks—was not a printer, and he told me as soon as he was introduced to me that the shop was to be closed immediately. He requested that I vacate the premises within a fortnight, and demanded to be shown my room so that he could see what might be made of it.

Unlike Mr. Priestland, Mr. Horrocks was immediately taken with the Kharshahar carpet. "That's an interesting item," he observed. "I presume that it's included with the fixtures."

"Of course," the solicitor said.

I protested, but in vain. The solicitor was armed with an inventory which included a carpet in my room, and a bed—for whose removal Horrocks suggested that I ought to be charged. Mr. Priestland had made no record of the originals being spoiled. Nor, of course, had I any receipt to prove that I had purchased the carpet, or even any account to offer of exactly where and when I had obtained it. I might have found witnesses to testify that I had put a carpet in store at Kimmeridge, and that I had taken it with me when I left, but that would only have led to further inquiries as to its origin.

I had no alternative but to take it away without permission, knowing that the removal would be calculated as a theft. I knew that I had to go a long way to avoid the possibility of pursuit, arrest and imprisonment, so I headed north and did not stop until I came to Cumberland.

I dared not look for work as a printer or a medical orderly, so I became a general handyman and kitchen assistant in a hotel in Keswick, in return for my board and a weekly pittance. It was enough; all I wanted was a place to lay my magic carpet so that I might complete its redemption—but such was my anxiety that my dreams turned from misery to terror once again. Their hard-won amorphousness was replaced by materials of an intensely personal nature.

I dreamed that I met Pemberly, and that he stamped upon my face with his army boot, no less forcibly for the want of a fulcrum. I dreamed that I met Radland, and that he stabbed me in the guts with a carpet-knife. I dreamed that I met Priestland, and that he shit all over me and turned my flesh putrid. I dreamed that I met Horrocks, who brought policemen and bailiffs to carry out his furious orders. I dreamed that I met my mother...and had far rather it had been my father, even if he were leading an army of wrathful angels.

I did not know, at first, whether this was merely another phase in my redemption of the carpet or a setback in my mission. Eventually, I was forced to admit that the latter was more likely—but that only made me determined to redouble my efforts. I began to answer my phantom persecutors, not with active resistance but with calm, counsel and forgiveness, but dream-Pemberly continued to rain his impossible kicks upon me, and dream-Priestland continued to decay before my eyes, and my dream-mother wept so fearfully that...all of which would have been nothing but a temporary setback, I feel sure, if....

Everything would have worked out perfectly had I not looked into a mirror one day in September, while fully conscious and about my legitimate business, sweeping the corridor on the second floor, and realized that my face was blurred.

I had to put my nose to the glass to see the clouding that had begun to overtake my left eye. Some mysterious blight had spread from its useless counterpart.

I continued to ply my broom as best I could, but when I came to wash the dishes after dinner I broke three glasses, and had to confess to the cook that I was no longer competent to do my work.

That night, for the first and last time, I tried to trace the carpet's maze with my finger. I held to the track for three full hours, but I could not complete the course. My dreams that night were all of colour, fire, and glory, but when I woke in the morning I was blind to the actual world.

The hotelier wanted to be rid of me without delay, and there was only one thing I could do. I gave him leave to write to my father—who is, after all, a Christian. While I was sighted, the Vicar of Stukeley had refused even to look at me; now that I was blind, he could not refuse to take me in. Nor did he, although he would not come to fetch me.

* * * * * *

I BEGGED THE hotelier to send my carpet with me when I set out on my journey home, and he promised faithfully to do it. Something certainly traveled with me, rolled and wrapped in an oilskin, and I am certain that I never took my hand off it, in the trap or on the train, even when I feel asleep—but I was cheated somewhere en route, more likely at the beginning than the end.

The hotelier swore, of course, that he had done exactly what I asked of him, and when my father was called upon to judge the carpet that was rolled out in my room he swore by God and all the angels that it was exactly as I described it to him—but they could not fool me. I am blind, but not an idiot.

"It's hideous, Arthur," my father said, "fit only for the company of a blind man." But he did not know what he was saying.

My father insists to this very day that the carpet on which I sleep is the one that I brought from Keswick, and that the carpet I brought from Keswick was the carpet I took to Keswick, but I know differently. I know that the carpet which sits beneath my bed is not the same, in shape, in texture or in quality as the marvel I had been briefly privileged to own. I know that the weaver of my dreams, laboriously repaired upon the loom of my soul, has been stolen, and that all the magic of my life has been stolen within it.

There is nothing remotely tender or sensuous in the caresses of the carpet that lies beneath me now—perpetually, for I never go out any more. There is no more luxury or promise in that coarse indifference than there is in my father's bleak resentment of my presence in the world.

My father says that he does not hate me now that I am all that is left to him, and that he has forgiven my betrayal of everything that he and God hold dear. It is not true, but I cannot care. Nor can I dream, by day or by night. There is nothing in my sleep but the moonless night of forgetfulness, and nothing in my days but an awareness of my own futility. Once, I lived in the borders of a great empire, to which I brought a kindly light. Now, I live in the margin of the world of horrid men, in which I am nothing.

I know that I could have reversed the spoliation of the Kharshahar carpet if only I had been given the chance to continue my efforts. Blindness of the sort that now afflicts me would have been no handicap. Such work is the work of a lifetime rather than a year, but it can be done; all it requires is the right man and a proper sense of purpose. I am that man, and have not the slightest hesitation in writing in the present tense. I am as sane as I ever was, as the continued ire and spite of my pious father will readily testify.

My face is spoiled, and my eyesight too, but the man who dwells within a shell of flesh is master of a realm where there is neither ugliness nor incapacity. If my soul is hurt, it is because I have lost my magic carpet and the opportunity to cure its malady. The wounds inflicted by the war could not have diminished me at all, if I were only able to weave my dreams with art and authority. In my mind's secret eye I see the truth more clearly than you could ever believe—and that truth would surely set me free, if only I could summon the empires of the carpet to my relief.

There is no longer magic in the weave of my life. I move mechanically through my sterile days. Once, I could have imagined no Hell worse than living as I now do. But I remember very vividly the days and nights when I had one good eye, and was able to tread so softly upon the gentle pile of my magic carpet. I am grateful for that memory, and I live within it as much and as best I can.

DEGREES OF SEPARATION

(written with John B. Ford)

WHEN THEY DIVORCED, my mother and father worked out the terms of their own separation. They split everything right down the middle, including us.

I always knew I had a brother, of course, but I never knew for sure whether he was an identical twin or a fraternal one. After all, we were only five weeks old when we were parted. My mother told me that we had looked alike, but that there had been some slight differences in our behavior. She had formed the distinct impression, albeit on very little evidence, that he "took after my father" and was a "right little bugger". Needless to say, she had also formed the complementary impression that I "took after her", and was therefore much to be preferred. She loved me very dearly, as I loved her. With my father gone, I was her only comfort and joy.

When I was six years old I asked my mother about her past, but my questions were so obviously disturbing that I never raised the subject again, although the meager information I obtained then raised more questions than it answered. My mother told me that the marriage had never been happy, and that my father was a cold and neglectful man who spent less and less time at home as time went by. When I asked her where he went—because I wanted to know where he had gone after the divorce, and where he and my brother were at that moment—she misunderstood me.

"To the slums," she said, meaning that that was where my father had gone rather than stay at home with her. "To some filthy floozy, I suppose."

We were poor, of course, but we were never miserable. Although it made her deeply sad to think of the past my mother was always cheerful when contemplating the future. "Everything will work out," she used to say. It was one of her favorite sayings. "Just give it a chance, and everything will work out". She was living proof that a person could escape the burden of the past and live in hope.

I tried. I was, after all, supposed to take after her. The possibility that my parents had mixed us up, so that each had taken charge of the one that took after the other, was too horrible for either of us to contemplate.

As I grew to maturity I resolved, for my mother's sake, that I must take every precaution to ensure that my life did not mirror my father's, or that of the brother who took after him. I knew this might be difficult, given that I had no idea where they were or what they were doing—my father never contacted us again once he and my brother had gone, presumably to live with his filthy floozy—but the necessary strategy seemed straightforward enough.

I knew that if my brother had been a fraternal twin no significant problem was likely to arise; the calculus of fate would ensure that his actions and mine would be uncorrelated. The danger lay in the possibility that we were identical, in which case our inner natures would be forever tempting us to seize similar opportunities and make similar mistakes. I knew that if this were the case, I had to make certain that I did not follow the promptings of my inner nature—but all I had to do in order to break the invisible psychic bonds which might or might not be tying my destiny to his, it seemed to me, was to attend carefully to my every spontaneous impulse, and then do something completely different.

I had not long grown into adulthood when I became certain that I must indeed be one of a pair of identical twins, for hardly a day passed by when I was free of strongly contrasting impulses. Although I tried hard to abide by the lessons which my loving mother had taught me, I was constantly aware of impulses pulling me in an altogether different direction. There was no way to explain it but to admit that I must still be psychically bonded to my twin—and that my twin must be a very nasty person indeed.

The psychological emanations of my evil twin were unrelenting. As I grew from my teens to my twenties I was constantly assailed by the most hideously violent impulses. I couldn't walk along a busy street without wanting to stab the people who accidentally strayed into my path. I learned to drive long before the notion of "road rage" became fashionable, but I never had a moment's peace from its angry promptings. In my work as a bank clerk—and later as a junior manager—I was continually tormented by the urge to steal huge sums of money.

147

When I married, it was only by exercising the utmost restraint that I was able to refrain from wife-battering and uxoricide, and I was glad in the end that my wife divorced me on the grounds of unreasonable behavior. She had never understood me, and her pleasant exterior hid a cold and neglectful person. I found that out almost as soon as we were wed, when she callously denied me the support I so desperately needed after my mother died of breast cancer. Unfortunately, even mourning could not distract me from my relentless tussle with evil. If anything, it intensified my second-hand passions—paradoxically, given that my evil twin could not have known that the mother who gave him birth had perished in ignominious agony.

* * * * * * *

AS TIME WENT by and my grief lessened, my battle with evil became less heated, though no less determined. The reduction of fervor was a good thing, because it gave me mental space to consider my tactics more carefully, but there was no let up in the pressure to which I was constantly subject. Every time my heart leapt as I saw the report of a violent incident in the *Daily Mail* I thought: "I bet my twin had a hand in that!" Every time my stomach churned as the disappearance of a young girl was reported on the BBC's *Six O'clock News* I said, silently: "She's dead—and my brother is responsible."

By the time I was thirty-three, in line for my own branch, I could bear these complex stresses and strains no longer. I knew that I had to find my evil twin, to see what could be done about the blight he had laid upon my life. I had no alternative but to hire a private detective to assist me, although the fees I was quoted were utterly outrageous, until good fortune guided me to Mr. Burke.

Mr. Burke was a strange little man with abnormal facial features, who took taciturnity to such unusual lengths that his long silences had a tomblike quality about them. He also had a very peculiar bald head which always reminded me somewhat of an egg. His peculiar appearance and manner presumably accounted for the fact that his fees were so inexpensive by comparison with the norms of his profession, but I felt sure from the moment I met him that he was a very good man—a man of wisdom and undoubtable honesty.

After assiduous searching, Mr. Burke discovered that my brother was the vicar of an inner-city parish. He was famed for his kindness, his charity and his tirelessness. He had been happily married for many years, and was the father of two lovely twin girls. I might have concluded that we must have been fraternal twins after all, but for the fact that photographs taken by Mr. Burke testified that we were as physically alike as two peas in a pod.

It was obvious what had happened. Like me, my brother must have been haunted by the idea that he had a twin somewhere—and like me, he had decided to distance himself from that twin by making sure that he defied the promptings of his own inner nature. The only difference between us was that he had gone to a much further extreme. While I, who had been brought up in a loving home by an eternal optimist, had been content to labor in the Temple of Mammon, he, who had been raised by a cold and neglectful man and a painted whore, had thrown himself desperately into the arms of Mother Church.

I wondered whether I ought to go to my brother and reveal myself, in order to explain how we had become what we were, but I decided against it. It wasn't that I was ashamed to admit to him that I had not succeeded as well as he, but that I was afraid of the effect the revelation might have on him. Once he knew the truth, might he not cease to suppress his violent and wicked urges, and cease to be the admirable man he was?

I couldn't be responsible for that. I stayed away.

Unfortunately, I didn't immediately consider the possibility that he might have come looking for me as I had gone looking for him, and found a disillusionment even deeper than mine. I was also slow to realize that, having gone to such an unreasonable extreme, he might one day suffer a reversal that would throw him back to the opposite so deeply ingrained in his nature. By the time I found him, alas, both these things had happened. Beneath his seemingly-blameless exterior the rot had set in—and once having taken hold of him, had transformed him inwardly into a duplicate of his father.

He had never forgiven me, you see, for winning his mother's love. Vicar or not, he had never been able to accept that I was the better man. If only he hadn't found out that I knew, he might have been able to keep up the facade forever, but when he discovered what I was—and that I'd come looking for him—he must have known that the game was up.

It was the faithful Mr. Burke who explained all this to me, in his own quiet way. It was he who made me see that I had to expose my brother for what he really was. I had to locate his filthy floozy, so that his loving wife would see him for what he really was. Mr. Burke's photographs revealed that she looked exactly like my mother. When I saw them it was all I could do to avoid breaking down in tears.

Just give it a chance, my mother would have said, and everything will work out. Mr. Burke was on the case, and I knew that everything previously hidden would now come to light. I had every confidence that everything would work out for the very best.

* * * * * * *

NOW THAT I knew there had to be a floozy involved I wasn't at all surprised when Mr. Burke showed me photographs of a certain building to which my brother paid frequent visits. The report he gave me to read was very thorough and extensive, and I knew that I would need time to digest it, so I poured him a double whisky and supplied the straw he needed to drink it.

The report informed me that the building was to be found in the heart of the worst slum area of the city: a red-light district where prostitution was rife. And drugs, I had to suppose; drugs were easily obtainable in all such places. When I expressed this opinion, Mr. Burke was quick to agree.

I readily deduced that my brother, as a vicar, would probably use his religious duties to mask his clandestine visits to his floozy. Drug overdoses, death from AIDS and drug-related murders would obviously be very common among the population of that part of the city. The administration of the last rites would provide his passport to visit his fancy piece. How very easy it would be for a man posing as a vicar to conceal his seedy little excursions with all manner of pious diversions! In the name of the Lord he would set forth beneath a cloak of apparent love and devotion, ostensibly ministering to the suffering of the many, stealthily intruding the conviction into the minds of all observers that he was a good Christian soldier intent on doing battle with all manner of pestilence and corruption. But it was perfectly obvious to me—and to the invaluable Mr. Burke—that this particular soldier was intent on wielding a weapon of a very different kind, to the end of his own selfish pleasure. And so we went forth on a mission of our own, under cover of darkness.

We took Mr. Burke's red Ford Escort rather than my black Volvo, because the occasion seemed more red than black. Death was merely the cover that my brother employed; sex was undoubtedly his motive. Mr. Burke was whistling a funeral dirge through the pencil-thin hole he had made of his mouth as we followed my brother's motorcycle through the city. I thought at first that the detective had been influenced by the pervasive atmosphere of the slums, but I eventually began to wonder whether he might have some other reason for whistling that somber tune.

Paradoxically, though, we were both quite happy. We were convinced that we had successfully tracked down my brother's filthy floozy, and that we were about to catch him red-handed while he stole forbidden fruit. I actually tapped my foot and smiled while I hummed along to the tune of that funeral dirge!

Soon enough, my brother's motorcycle took a sharp left turn into a grimy alley. There was insufficient room for Mr. Burke's red Escort to follow. I couldn't help wondering whether my evil twin knew that he was being followed, and by whom. Perhaps the bond we had formed at birth was working to his advantage. Perhaps his theological training, although doubtless a mere pretence, had somehow enabled him to further enhance the hidden power of extra-sensory perception which links all identical twins one to another. I couldn't be sure, but the idea that my twin might have tuned into my brainwaves so accurately that he knew my innermost thoughts made me anxious.

We had no alternative but to park Mr. Burke's Escort next to the alley's entrance, and then to run with all possible speed in the direction of my brother's disappearing motorcycle. Alas, we had no hope of catching up—and to make matters worse, I was periodically forced to stop and wait for Mr. Burke. His frail and stumpy legs couldn't keep up with mine.

When we approached the end of the alley I was already resigned to the loss of our quarry, but my brain was suddenly filled with a queer tingling feeling, and although there was no audible noise I seemed to hear the totally incongruous sound of an eggshell being cracked. Perhaps, I thought, the nearness of my brother had increased my latent ability to exploit the secret store of extra-sensory perceptions within my own mind.

Turning to my right, I saw an extraordinarily dilapidated house with a small garage at the side. I recognized it immediately as the one I had seen in Mr. Burke's photographs, but the reality of it seemed far more sinister than its image.

"He's in there," I said to Mr. Burke. "I can sense the evil stench of his mind!"

We walked to the garage and passed through a narrow gap where the rusty-hinged double doors had not quite closed. We took out our torches and illuminated the inside of the building. Sure enough, one wheel of my brother's motorcycle protruded from beneath a couple of black shrouds that had been hastily draped over it. A wooden box filled with similar shrouds was located nearby, all of them black and all of them folded very neatly, ready for future use.

151

The light of my torch discovered a door allowing admission to the house.

"He's inside," I said to Mr. Burke. "A room on the upper floor. Oh, the horror!" Mr. Burke nodded to encourage me to go on, but said nothing.

The door opened on to a carpetless corridor strewn with the recumbent bodies of crack-addicts and meths drinkers. There was a strange, rather foul chemical odor saturating the atmosphere within the house. I couldn't tell, at first, whether the supine bodies were already dead or whether they had merely begun to decay prematurely. All were unmoving, and neither I nor Mr. Burke had any wish to touch them intimately in order to determine their exact status. When I asked Mr. Burke what he thought he began once again to whistle a mournful funeral dirge through the pencil-hole of his mouth.

As we walked along the corridor, the light of our torches showed me that some of the people distributed about its floor had grotesque facial wounds. It appeared that certain features— sometimes noses, sometimes eyes, and sometimes ears—had been surgically removed. All those who had been subjected to operations of this kind were clad in black shrouds.

This is all very curious, I thought to myself. *Is there no limit to the depths of my brother's depravity?* I was certain that my brother must be directly or indirectly responsible for the condition of all of these people. But where was his floozy?

At the far end of the corridor we passed through another door, then came to the foot of a wooden stairway. At this point, Mr. Burke whistled softly and tugged at my sleeve to attract my attention. He pointed downwards with the smooth white index finger of his right hand, and I saw that the dust on each step had been disturbed, leaving the imprints of a pair of shoes identical to my own. It was clear evidence that my brother had gone this way, sneaking up the stairway like an assassin. I had no doubt at all that he had a floozy upstairs, and began to wonder how many others there were to be discovered in similarly ugly dwellings.

Mr. Burke shook his hairless head slowly, in apparent disgust. He let loose a low whistle to signify his utter contempt for my brother. I realized that our mission was nearing its climax.

"Come on, Mr. Burke," I whispered. "We must catch the rat with his weapon unsheathed. Do you have your camera ready?"

We continued ascending the staircase until we reached the top floor of the house, then crept along a musty corridor until we came to a series of doors. As we passed the fifth door my brain tingled so sharply that I couldn't help imagining that acid was pouring into it. Mr. Burke looked up at me with some concern as I bit my fist in order to prevent myself screaming—but after exactly five seconds the pain passed. That was one second for each door we had passed. I had no doubt that Mr. Burke had also noticed this. He was a good detective, even if he did work cheap. He let out a little snort of pleasure as I looked at him approvingly.

"This is it," I whispered. "My brother and his floozy must be inside."

I took two paces back from the door, then hurled myself forward to strike it with my left shoulder—but my whole body was filled with a terrible pain and darkness descended upon my eyes as soon as I made contact with it.

* * * * * * *

ACCORDING TO MR. Burke, I remained unconscious for exactly five seconds. He succeeded in reviving me by whistling the tune of an uplifting hymn into my right ear. Wincing with pain, I thought for a moment that my shoulder was dislocated, but, if it had been, then Mr. Burke had already succeeded in replacing the bone in its socket. I thanked him very kindly.

Mr. Burke's tiny hand closed upon the handle of the door, and I felt quite ashamed of myself when I saw him open it very easily. I got to my feet immediately, eager to watch as Mr. Burke took a photograph of my brother engaged in some filthy act with his floozy— but the sight that met my eyes was not at all what I had expected.

The room was equipped as a laboratory of some kind.

Test tubes and vials filled with bubbling chemicals were being steadily heated by Bunsen burners, while blue and green gases floated through the air, like clouds of living intelligence gazing down from the ceiling with evil intent. On the floor there was a selection of shrouded corpses, all of which had been operated upon in some sickening way or other. Some had been reduced to little more than torsos with only a single arm or leg attached. I notice three porcine carcasses, and remembered that a sudden outbreak of pig thefts had recently been mentioned on the *Six O'clock News*.

But there was no sign of my evil twin.

At the far side of the room there was a door to a balcony, which stood ajar. I realized that my brother must have detected my approaching presence and had made a hasty escape even before I hurled myself at the door, perhaps taking his floozy with him. Presumably, she posed as a laboratory assistant to some insane genius

153

condemned to work in the slums since being struck off by the General Medical Council.

I looked round for Mr. Burke, intent on sharing this new theory with him, but I couldn't see any sign of him at first. Eventually, I perceived him standing in a dim-lit corner, his torch playing upon a peculiar oval object. He seemed to be held fast, in some kind of trance. When I drew nearer I could hear him emitting little grunts of amazement through his nose.

I added the strength of my flashlight to his own fading beam, intent on gaining a better view of whatever it was that fascinated him—and gasped in astonishment to see that it was a large black egg. It was standing upright, but had been broken open, as if something had recently hatched out from it. Attached to the top and base of the egg was an assortment of tubes and wires. It seemed to me that whatever creature had been maturing within had been artificially stimulated into life, although it must have been possessed by its own urge to seek freedom. If my brother had had anything to do with the influences visited upon the egg's occupant, I thought, the hatchling might have done better to fight and conquer that urge!

When I turned to Mr. Burke I noticed that tears were running from his strange eyes. It was as if looking at the egg had whipped up some long-forgotten memory within him. He took a step forward, and for a moment I thought he was actually going to climb inside the egg shell. I realized that it would have been a very good fit.

Through the open door that let out on to the balcony came the sudden sound of an engine being revved. I ran to the balcony, and arrived just in time to look down and see the hateful sight of my brother's motorcycle roaring away into the night. Seated behind him on the pillion was a small man who thrust two pale fingers up in the air at me.

Save for the obvious fact that he was naked, he appeared to be identical to Mr. Burke.

* * * * * * *

MR. BURKE WAS really never quite the same after this strange sequence of incidents. I became so worried about him that I allowed him to move into my house. He was obviously very disturbed, but he would not give me the slightest clue concerning the source of his distress. I had to work it out for myself.

Mr. Burke was obviously a twin, like me, but for some unaccountable reason his twin had remained dormant throughout his life, cocooned within an egg. What bliss it must have been to be Mr.

Burke! Unlike me, he must have spent his entire life bathed in psychic emanations of a paradisal quality, broadcast by an intelligence that had never known wakefulness, let alone misery. Although physically divided, as all twins are—even those who are never separated by divorce—Mr. Burke and his twin had maintained the ultimate psychic harmony. The twin in the egg would, of course, have received his own flow of second-hand experience from Mr. Burke, but could only experience it as a dream, enigmatic and beautifully surreal. What a perfect relationship the two had had! Until now.

Everything had changed, and all because of me. If I had never hired Mr. Burke to find my brother, he would never have found his own. If I had never insisted that Mr. Burke must lead me to my brother's hidey-hole, the egg would never have been broken. Now, everything was different. Paradise was lost, and Mr. Burke had been cast into the same existential inferno that I had suffered all my life.

How could I have known? I couldn't, of course—but that didn't make me feel any less responsible.

I knew now that I had underestimated my brother, and that my mother had underestimated my father. She had assumed that he was cold and neglectful towards her because he had a mistress, because she had taken it for granted that he was a man whose passions, though degraded, were essentially natural. In fact, his coldness and neglect reflected a much deeper sickness of the soul. He was a mad scientist, not in the trivial sense that he was a scientist who happened to be mad, but in the tragically pathological sense that he was a sincere and committed practitioner of *mad science*. My brother had indeed taken after him. His careful disguise as a man of the cloth was more sinister in its hypocrisy than I had previously dared to imagine. Perhaps he did have a floozy, and perhaps she did serve as his laboratory assistant, but she was a superficial element of his real sin.

In contemplating what I now knew to be my evil twin's true nature I was, of course, tempted to describe him as a Frankenstein, but I was well aware of the fact that Frankenstein's subtitle had identified him as a modern Prometheus, intent on stealing the fire of the gods. My brother, I felt sure, would be better described as a modern Epimetheus, intent on opening a new Pandora's box, from which he would release another swarm of evils upon the world. Yes, he was a Frankenstein—but he was the darker of the Frankenstein twins—and the first victim of his new swarm of evils was Mr. Burke, condemned now to bear the horrors of his own twin's conscious existence.

Mr. Burke hardly whistled at all in the weeks that followed our fateful excursion, save for one sad occasion that I remember with particular vividness.

It was a balmy summer night, when the air in the house was so close that I had to sleep with the bedroom windows open. I was awakened from sleep by the sound of an odd keening that seemed to come from the garden below my bedroom. So deep and melancholy was the quality of this sound that a lump formed in my throat and tears of grief welled in my tired eyes for the first time since my mother had died.

I got out of bed and put on my dressing-gown and slippers. Then I went downstairs to investigate. I knew that it could only be Mr. Burke out there in the garden, but I was concerned about him. I had grown very fond of Mr. Burke; I had grown to treasure his odd little whistles and the silent messages he would relay to me by gesture. He was more than a detective to me now.

There was a full moon that night, although I doubt that it had anything to do with Mr. Burke's bizarre behavior. I saw that he was naked, standing with his back towards me on the edge of the lawn, next to a flowerbed. Around him on the grass he had placed five free-range eggs, which he had taken from the pantry.

As I grew nearer I noticed that part of the flowerbed had been churned up as if by a gargantuan mole. I started with alarm as I remembered that I had buried my pet spaniel, King Charles, at that very spot six months before.

I approached Mr. Burke just as a particularly mournful whistling noise fell from his lips, only to die upon the silence of the night. "Come back to bed, Mr. Burke," I said, very softly. "You'll be arrested if you carry on like this."

There was a dull thud as something was released from Mr. Burke's cradling arms. I saw the corpse of my former pet lying on the grass. When Mr. Burke eventually turned round to face me, I saw that tears of sadness were trickling down his face. The strange whistling which began to emanate uncertainly from his pencil-hole of a mouth sounded like sobbing, albeit of a kind that was barely half-human. He had been such a cheerful, hopeful, honest and businesslike man, and now he was reduced to this!

It was only when the electric light from the kitchen window fell upon Mr. Burke's body that I had my first clear view of his naked form, for we had been very careful to respect one another's privacy since he had moved in. I saw something which intrigued me greatly: upon Mr. Burke's chest was what appeared to be the deep scar of a major surgical operation—but it had been expertly carved into the shape of the letter B.

* * * * * * *

MR. BURKE HAD obviously been unhinged by what he had witnessed during our recent mission to the red light district, but I began to wonder then whether he had been a little unbalanced even before he had ever entered into my employment. I wondered whether he might be an outcast from some secret society, and whether he had been communicating too much by his admittedly-unusual methods. Considering that he couldn't speak a single word, the Mr. Burke I had known before our expedition to the slums could be quite chatty at times.

After the incident with the spaniel I was forced to reconsider my whole relationship with Mr. Burke, and it occurred to me that what had happened at my brother's secret laboratory had been remarkably coincidental. Was it not stretching credulity a little too far, I wondered, to accept that my evil twin had merely happened to have a egg in his possession that contained the sleeping twin of the detective I had hired to find him? Must there not be some kind of pattern linking all our lives?

It was, perhaps, unfortunate that it wasn't until our professional relationship ripened into true friendship that I began to consider the possibility that Mr. Burke might somehow have been placed—unwittingly, I had no doubt—in the detective agency precisely in order that I might discover and employ him. After all, I reminded myself, there are a million ways in which a man's memory might be erased and replaced by a false one. We live in inventive times, and my father had obviously been an inventive man.

I became convinced, in the end, that Mr. Burke must have been a victim of hypnotism, but that his suppressed memories had now been resurrected into a strange half-life by the sight of the black egg. Whether or not that was the explanation of his strange behavior, however, it was plain to see that Mr. Burke was now a helpless and broken man, who stood in dire need of comfort, love and a purpose in life.

I knew then that we had to return to the house to which my brother had led us—not, after all, merely because he kept a floozy there, in the guise of a laboratory assistant or any other, but because he harbored a secret far deeper and darker than even I had dared to imagine.

* * * * * * *

FIVE DAYS AFTER the incident in the garden Mr. Burke and I set out again on our mission of discovery. This time we took the Volvo, because I was certain that this chapter of our adventure would be concerned with death and not with sex. We left early, at the break of dawn. I was determined that we would be early birds, fully equipped to catch the worm. As we drove into the slums, though, I could not help fantasizing that the worm in question would be an ice-cold floozy who wore a shroud for a nightgown, in preparation for a night that would last forever. I had no rest at all, and never would until my evil twin and I were somehow reconciled—or parted decisively and forever.

Six degrees of separation, it is said, are all that stand between any two members of the human race, selected at random. There is more genetic variation in a single troop of baboons than in the entire human population. We are far too close to one another as it is, and should not be required to bear the kind of intimacy that comes with being a twin. It is a kind of intimacy that is too intense to bear, especially in ignorance. The only kind of twin a man should have is the kind that sleeps in a black egg, destined never to suckle at a mother's loving but cancerous breast.

As I drove through the deserted streets Mr. Burke guided me, using high- and low-pitched whistle to indicate whether I should take left or right turns. By this method he was able to direct me to a high-rise block of flats entirely populated with junkies, single mothers, joy riders, and whores. If my brother's floozy worked as a laboratory assistant at the other house we had visited, this was obviously her home address. We pulled up at the kerb and stared up at the tower of sin.

"He's been here many a time," I confirmed. "He's here now, on the topmost floor."

Mr. Burke nodded his peculiar head solemnly. He was, of course, in touch with his own twin, and knew as well as I did where we must go. We left the car and entered the flats discreetly. I was astonished to find the lifts in good working order. When we traveled up to the top floor Mr. Burke began to whistle one of his funeral dirges, but I could tell that he wasn't very happy. He didn't look happy at all.

When we reached the top floor I took care to shorten my stride, falling into step with him as we marched unerringly to the door behind which our two brothers were concealed. Mr. Burke favored me with five little nods of approval as I measured out an appropriate number of steps for my shoulder charge. With fierce determination I rushed towards the door, smashing it open without feeling the slightest of pain. It was dark inside because the curtains were drawn shut, and Mr. Burke and I had to fumble for our torches. We flicked them on simultaneously.

There is no word to describe the kind of place it was. To my mind, *mortuary* signifies a sterile and sanitary place, and *charnel-house* does not deserve the indignities heaped upon it by writers of crude horror stories. At least half the corpses in the room appeared to have been disinterred from graves, to judge from their advanced state of decay and their appalling odor. At first I assumed that this overpowering stench was the reason why Mr. Burke ran out of the flat, snorting madly, but his hectic retreat might equally well have been prompted by the sight of all the swinish creatures that had been meticulously dismembered. Here, in what I presumed was his second home rather than his secret workplace my brother hadn't even bothered clothing his victims in shrouds. Perhaps, too, he believed that animal flesh was less important than human flesh.

There was no one living in the flat. My evil twin was not there. Nor was Mr. Burke's. Nor was the ice-cold floozy in the shroud-like nightgown.

I thought, when I finally tore myself away, that I would find Mr. Burke waiting for me outside, perhaps sitting on the bonnet of my black Volvo, snorting solemnly to himself. I was slightly hurt when I found that he wasn't, and also slightly concerned. I felt rather guilty that I had let him run off in such a distraught state, and then had waited so long before following him. But how else was I to obtain an accurate measurement of the extent of my evil twin's depravity? I had to be brave and thorough if I were ever to bring this matter to a satisfactory conclusion.

I began to search the infinitely depressing streets for my friend, even leaning out of the Volvo's window occasionally to ask the local early risers whether they had seen him. They spat at me by way of reply. I tried calling out his name once or twice, but that only attracted unwelcome attention. I wondered what else I could reasonably do. *Perhaps he has returned home on foot*, I thought. I had just made up my mind that this was the likeliest possibility, and was about to start my return journey, when I noticed one of Mr. Burke's files on the passenger seat. I opened it. Clipped to the first document, overlaying the text, was a Polaroid photograph of my brother's wife, the likeness to my beloved mother even more striking than usual. The semi-detached house where she lived with the man she thought of as a good clergyman was located in a prosperous

159

suburb not unlike the one where my own house was. I decided that the time had come to call on her, and to break the news that the husband she thought of was a saint was a murderer, a defiler of the dead, and a devotee of mad science.

****

I ASSUME THAT the house in which my brother and his wife lived was the property of the Church, although it was not what tradition would have defined as a vicarage. It was located in a different universe from the edifices I had visited in the company of Mr. Burke.

The garden was full of white roses but I could not catch their scent as I approached the front door. The door chime was unusually deep, but the suggestion of tolling church bells could only have been a fashionable irony. Through the frosted glass of the door I saw a slim, blurred figure approaching. I couldn't help wondering whether she had been lurking just inside one of the inner doors, waiting eagerly for someone—perhaps anyone—to call. I had no time for further flights of fancy, though. The door opened to reveal a younger version of my mother—a version younger than any I had ever been privileged to see, bathing in a glow of perfect health, radiating hope and optimism.

I bid her good morning and asked her if her husband was home. I smiled as I did it, imagining the surprise that she must be feeling as she looked at her husband's double and realized that the man she had married was but half of a previously-unsuspected whole—but she showed not the slightest flicker of recognition or astonishment. She merely informed me, politely, that her husband was busy supervising choir practice in another parish, substituting for a colleague who was ill."

I asked if I might step inside in order to import some valuable information to her. She told me that parishioners were never allowed into the house while her husband was absent.

I didn't argue. I had realized that there was something very odd about my brother's wife. Her voice sounded rather mechanical. Now that I looked at her more closely, I realized that the resemblance to my mother was not as strong as I had first thought. Her mouth, in particular, was quite different. Indeed, it appeared on close inspection to be slightly deformed, almost as if a row of small pencil-holes had been scissored into one. Red lipstick had been smeared over the lips, thickly enough to hide their abnormality, but at close range the scars were visible. I noticed, too, that her hair was dyed, and that she was wearing contact lenses.

I realized that it was not my brother's wife at all. It was his floozy, who had been made up to look like her. I realized that his wife must be dead—murdered, I had no doubt—and that this substitute had been carefully introduced into her place.

I begged her to listen to me, but she just looked at me with a peculiar glassy-eyed stare. At that moment I heard the sound of the Volvo's engine starting up. I turned around just in time to see someone who looked identical to me driving it away. As the car turned the corner the driver reached across in order to wave out of the nearside window, and he tooted the horn.

I knew then that he intended to steal my life as well as my soul, and complete the Hell that he had already made of it. He intended to leave all his crimes to me—everything, in fact, except his floozy, who steadfastly refused to recognize me. I knew that I had to find Mr. Burke, but I had no idea where to start looking.

* * * * * * *

BY THE TIME I had walked home the police were waiting to arrest me. They assured me that they had all the evidence they needed to convict me. The security cameras at my bank clearly showed me driving up in my own car and using my own keys to break through the security mechanisms—and if that were not enough, they had collected abundant samples of DNA that would put the issue beyond doubt. To make matters worse, the Volvo had mowed down five pedestrians while making its getaway. Acting on a tip-off, the police had subsequently raided a house and a flat situated in the worst the city's slums, and had found rooms that defied description—although the detective superintendent who interviewed me did make a valiant attempt, never once mentioning the word "charnel".

I was obviously a very sick man, the detective superintendent said, but that would only make it easier to lock me up for life.

They didn't believe me, at first, when I told them about my brother, but I knew they'd have to change their tune once they'd checked the birth certificates, and I knew that Mr. Burke would come forward to confirm everything that I'd said. He was my alibi, my ace in the hole. I didn't mind being remanded in custody, because I knew that it was only a matter of time before they released me and gave me my life back.

I didn't really want to watch the *Six O'clock News* with my fellow inmates in case there was an item about me that would stir up resentment, but curiosity got the better of me. I was glad that I did, firstly because there was a report of yet more thefts from pig farms in the main body of the news, and secondly because the humorous item at the end was about reported sightings of "whistling aliens" with bald heads and weird scars on their chests formed like letters of the English alphabet. The letter C was mentioned, and H, but not A or B. The reporters had obviously got hold of the wrong end of the stick, but it was a hopeful sign, because I knew that an investigation was now under way and that the truth would eventually come out.

I had a bad night, of course, alone in my cell, and the following morning didn't seem much better. I looked forward all day to the four o'clock appointment I had with my solicitor, because I was sure that he'd have some good news for me.

He told me that the police had now concluded their search of the flat that Mr. Burke and I had visited the previous morning, and had found among the many dead bodies one that was merely asleep. Even better, they had realized immediately that the living man fitted the description I had given them of Mr. Burke. I realized in my turn that Mr. Burke must have been ashamed of his sudden cowardly retreat from the flat, and must have gone back as soon as he had plucked up sufficient courage.

The police had tried to question Mr. Burke, my solicitor said, but they hadn't been able to get much out of him to begin with because the only sounds he was able to emit were porcine snorts and strange whistling sobs. He had, however, been as enthusiastic to establish communication with them as they were to establish communication with him. He had led them, in the course of that quest, to one of the animal corpses that had not yet been removed. He had embraced it fondly, before dipping his finger into the blood that had begun to leak from the curiously-formed wound in his chest, and then had painstakingly inscribed the word MOTHER on the gloss-painted door of the master bedroom.

I knew then that it was only a matter of time before the authorities figured out who was who and what was what, even if matters of how and why remained stubbornly mysterious—as, in my experience, they frequently do.

It's just as my mother always said. Everything will work out. I just have to give it a chance, and everything will work out.

Perhaps I've always been too close to the problem, and now that it's in other hands it can be put into its proper perspective. Objectivity can be a great asset in getting to grips with certain kinds of issues. Anyway, no matter what comes out of Pandora's box, hope is always there at the bottom, and you have to treasure it.

Everything will surely work out, if I give it a chance. After all, I haven't done anything wrong.

ABOUT THE AUTHOR

BRIAN STABLEFORD was born in Yorkshire in 1948. He taught at the University of Reading for several years, but is now a full-time writer. He has written many science fiction and fantasy novels, including: *The Empire of Fear, The Werewolves of London, Year Zero, The Curse of the Coral Bride,* and *The Stones of Camelot.* Collections of his short stories include: *Sexual Chemistry: Sardonic Tales of the Genetic Revolution, Designer Genes: Tales of the Biotech Revolution,* and *Sheena and Other Gothic Tales.* He has written numerous nonfiction books, including *Scientific Romance in Britain, 1890-1950, Glorious Perversity: The Decline and Fall of Literary Decadence,* and *Science Fact and Science Fiction: An Encyclopedia.* He has contributed hundreds of biographical and critical entries to reference books, including both editions of *The Encyclopedia of Science Fiction* and several editions of the library guide, *Anatomy of Wonder.* He has also translated numerous novels from the French language, including several by the feuilletonist Paul Féval.

www.ingramcontent.com/pod-product-compliance
Lightning Source LLC
Chambersburg PA
CBHW020645180626
46816CB00003B/1136